I0536390

DARE TO BREATHE

The Maxwell Series - Book 6

S.B. ALEXANDER

Raven Wing Publishing

Dare to Breathe
Book Six: The Maxwell Series
Copyright © 2018 by S.B. Alexander
All rights reserved.
First Edition:
E-book ISBN-13: 978-0-9989157-6-0
Print ISBN-13: 978-0-9989157-7-7

Visit: www.sbalexander.com
Editor: Red Adept Editing, www.redadeptediting.com
Cover Design by Hang Le: http://www.byhangle.com

This is a work of fiction. Names, characters, places and incidents either are the product of the author's imagination or are used fictitiously, and any resemblance to locales, events, business establishments, or actual persons-living or dead-is entirely coincidental.

Adult Content Warning: The content contained is the book includes adult language and sexual content. This book is intended for adult audiences 17 years of age and older.

CHAPTER 1
KADE

Trekking across campus, my stomach roiled as if I were riding fifty-foot waves. I didn't know why I was nervous. I was surprising the love of my existence, Lacey Robinson, the most beautiful girl I'd ever met and the one woman that I wanted to spend the rest of my life with. She was finally graduating college. The last four years had been hell, living approximately one hundred eighty-five miles from her.

Each and every time I'd come up to Maine to see her, it was the longest fucking drive in history. But the nerve-racking drive was mild compared to the lonely nights where I had to sleep alone, dreaming, thinking, and going out of my mind with her not at my side.

I swore my hair would be gray like my dad's by the time she graduated. Not only did I miss the fuck out of her, but I'd been frightened that her PTSD would get the best of her and that I wouldn't be around to help like I had when we were teenagers.

I hadn't even wanted to drum up our senior year in high school. Nor did I want to remember that night her car had broken down just after I'd met her. I'd given her a ride home, and as soon as I'd pulled into her driveway, she'd jumped out of my truck and thrown herself at her garage door before blacking out. Then there was the time she had been trying out for the boys' high school baseball team and had fallen flat on her face mid pitch and blacked out.

After high school graduation, I hadn't wanted her to leave for college. I'd wanted her to stay in Ashford. I'd wanted her with me. But I couldn't suffocate her and didn't want to, either. Regardless, when she'd made her decision to attend Colby College in Maine, I swore she'd torn my heart out of my chest.

"I need to prove I can live on my own. You and my dad won't be far. We can visit on weekends," she'd said in her sexy voice that had been embedded in my psyche since the day I'd met her.

A chill hung in the morning air as the sun crept up the skyline. Students hurried in all directions with backpacks on their shoulders, phones in their hands, and barely a smile on their faces.

I, on the other hand, grinned as wide as I could at the notion that I was about to have my girl back in my arms forever.

Her graduation was scheduled for the next day, and I was about to do something I'd been dying to do since I'd met her—propose. I'd wanted to wait until I had enough money to buy the ring. I'd scrimped and saved every penny I could after paying for rent and other living expenses. Mr. Robinson paid me a decent salary for managing his club, Rumors, in Boston. But with the cost of living high in the New England area, money didn't go far, which was why I'd moved back home and into the boathouse after Kody had moved in with his girl-friend, Jessie. I'd also convinced Mr. Robinson to let me manage his new club in Ashford, although I hadn't needed to twist his arm since he'd opened up a new record label in Boston and didn't have time to oversee the Cave.

Nevertheless, my heart beat like a bucking bronco. I couldn't wait to wrap my arms around my girl, bring her home, make passionate love to her, and tell her over and over again—morning, noon, and night—how much I loved the crap out of her.

A humungous oak tree sat in front of Lacey's dorm, masking part of the stone facade that reminded me of something from medieval times. I was about to take a right down the winding path, when my vision blurred. I came to an abrupt halt and blinked several times before an excruciating pain gripped the back of my head. Fucking migraine was about to start. I took in a large breath, when a guy wearing thick, purple-framed glasses came toward me. At least I thought it was a dude.

"Kade, is that you? Are you okay?" the girl asked, settling in front of me.

I blinked again to make sure I wasn't hallucinating. Sometimes with my migraines, my brain didn't fire on all cylinders. I inhaled the sweet scent of flowering blooms that wafted in the June air, briefly closed my eyes, then oriented my vision.

The *he* was definitely a *she,* and one of Lacey's friends that I barely remembered meeting over the years.

Her brown eyes sparkled as she smiled up at me. "You look like you're about to pass out. Can I call Lacey for you?"

Hell no. Lacey was the last person that needed to know I had a migraine, only because I didn't want to ruin the moment. "I'm good. Thank you." I stared at her, trying to remember her name.

As though she knew my struggle, she said, "I'm Jennifer. We met several months back."

Then it clicked. Lacey had talked about Jennifer and two of her other friends that she always hung out with after classes or when she had time.

I didn't want to be rude, but making small talk, or talking at all, seemed like a feat in itself with my head throbbing. So I smiled at her.

She lightly touched my arm. "Are you sure you don't need me to call Lacey?"

3

I staved off a wince from the throbbing in my head. "I'm good." *Total lie.*

Nodding, she bounced off to wherever she was going.

I took in a large breath then let it out before I rubbed the back of my head. My migraines had been few and far between over the years. As of late though, the headaches seemed to be returning more frequently. I chalked them up to my worry over proposing to Lacey. *Is the ring designed perfectly? Would she like it? Fuck. Would she say yes?* She wanted to play baseball more than anything in the world. She'd hoped that one day a major league team would sign her. In my book, seeing a female play in the major leagues would be so freaking cool. I wanted that female to be Lacey, yet I didn't. She would always be on the road. It would be hard to start a family. I doubted that she could pitch while she was pregnant, which meant that having kids might not be an option in the near future.

Then again, I was getting ahead of myself. Lacey hadn't mentioned anything about any team being interested in her. Regardless, whether a team was or not, I could still propose. We could still get married.

With the migraine intensifying, I started once again for Lacey's dorm. The headache wasn't going to stop me from the reason I'd shown up a day early. I'd thought about how, when, and where I would get down on one knee and ask her to be my bride. I'd thought about popping the big question to her on a baseball field, but I didn't want to associate her love of baseball for the love we had for each other. Sure, the place would be special to her, but not necessarily to me. The way I saw us, was just that—*us.* I'd decided two nights ago that simple was best—no fancy restaurant and no frills.

When I cleared the oak tree, I almost lost my lunch. I blinked hard, trying to make sure that the six-foot dude pressing his body up against my girl wasn't real. Talk about a fucking distraction. I couldn't move an inch down the path, nor did I see anyone or anything in my peripheral vision.

I slipped a hand into my right jeans pocket and gripped the small box that contained the precious stone. My headache grew to enormous proportions. I didn't want to think the worst, but I did, especially when the blond dude rubbed her back, playing with my girl's long hair that spilled down to her ass—the same ass I'd had my hands on last weekend and every weekend for the last month.

The dude gripped the sides of her arms then whispered something in her ear. From where I stood, it looked as though he was nibbling on her earlobe. My body went ramrod straight. *Kill the fucker* was on repeat in my head. I closed my hands into fists, my nails digging into my skin.

In slow motion, Lacey turned. Shock jumped off her as she locked eyes with me. For several beats, none of us moved. I sifted through my memory to recall if she'd given me any signs that she was seeing someone else. I came up empty—zilch, nothing. Our relationship had never been tighter. Our lovemaking was off the charts and better than ever. She'd always been elated to see me if we'd gone a minute without seeing each other. Hell, one day without seeing each other, and we were like two horny rabbits. But at that moment, she wasn't running into my arms like she usually did. She wasn't smiling or beaming at me with love in those green eyes that always reminded me of a lush meadow on a spring day.

My heart fell to my feet. I shouldn't jump to conclusions. But that was me. I always thought the worst. I always fought then asked questions later. I wouldn't have been freaking the fuck out if she'd smiled or run into my arms. Maybe then I wouldn't have been thinking that the dude who was again whispering something in her ear was having his way with my girl.

Lacey rolled back her shoulders and said something to Blondie. He nodded then ambled away with a satisfied grin on his face.

Biting her lip, she walked toward me in what seemed like slow motion. I knew her tells inside and out, and that lip biting screamed that she was guilty and worried.

Her throat bobbed as she lifted up on her toes to kiss me. "I thought you were coming up tonight." Her voice was low and reserved.

I edged back before her lips touched mine. "Who's the dude?" I flicked my chin at the retreating backside of the blond guy.

She huffed as she took one step back. "Randy. He's a friend and a classmate." She poked me in the chest. "Before you get even more jealous, nothing is going on. He was wishing me luck."

I cocked an eyebrow. She'd never mentioned her friend Randy. Sure, she had talked about Jennifer and, I thought, a Diane or Peggy or Heather or all of them. Honestly, I hardly paid much attention to conversation when Lacey and I got together after not seeing each other for weeks on end. "Luck for what?"

A girl called to Lacey. "Are you coming to the party tonight?"

Lacey glimpsed Jennifer, who was approaching.

When Jennifer sidled up to Lacey, she asked me, "How are you feeling?"

Lacey angled her head at me. "Feeling?"

Jennifer flicked her short brown hair from her face. Now that I could see clearer, I did recall meeting Jennifer a time or two when I'd come up to visit Lacey.

A crease formed on Lacey's forehead. "What's Jennifer talking about?"

"Nothing," I said in a clipped tone. It wasn't that I didn't want to tell her about my migraine. I wanted to know more about what she was hiding, and she was hiding something.

Jennifer hiked her bag over her shoulder. "He looked pale when I saw him a few minutes ago just before he turned down to your dorm. Anyway, I forgot something in my dorm room. Lacey, try to make it tonight and bring your hunk of a man." She winked at me then giggled as she rushed down to the three-story building.

Lacey stuck her hands on her hips. "You still look a little pale. Are you here to give me bad news? Did something happen to my dad? Your family?"

Oh, fuck. The conversation and the reason I was there were all going to shit.

I shook my head vigorously. "I didn't come with bad news. I came to surprise my girl." Instead she was the one surprising me. The pain in the back of my head intensified, and as much as I needed to sit down, I wanted to get to the heart of why Randy was snuggling with her. "If Randy was wishing you luck, then why was he rubbing your back like he was in love with you or consoling you?"

She checked her watch. "I have to meet my coach. I haven't told you yet, but Coach got news yesterday that a major league team is interested in me." Her eyes widened. "Can you believe it?"

My eyebrows shot up to my hairline. I should be swinging her around and kissing her. But with my migraine, Randy, and the guilt that had settled in her eyes, I needed to know what she was hiding. Besides, she didn't sound all that happy, and for that, I had to pause. This was Lacey Robinson, the girl I loved, who lived and breathed baseball.

"Why don't you sound excited?" I asked.

She studied me for the longest minute. "Let me meet with my coach. You can come with. Then we can talk."

Acid settled in my stomach. I didn't like her tone. It was as though she was about to tell me she wanted to break up with me. Or maybe my migraine was clouding my senses.

I snaked my arm around her waist and drew her to me. Immediately, my body reacted in all the right places. I lowered my head until our lips were a hair apart. "Go talk to your coach. Then meet me at the bed and breakfast. I'm in the same room I always stay in." I didn't have many choices of hotels in the small town. It was either the bed and breakfast or the motel, and Lacey liked the bed and breakfast.

She brushed her lips over mine. "I love you. I'm not cheating."

A slight breeze picked up, sending a chill down my arms.

I searched her eyes for answers. All I found was love. "I know." Even though that nagging, doubtful voice in my head made me ques-

7

tion things, I did believe her. She wouldn't throw away what we had, which was the deepest love any two humans could have for each other. "I don't like his hands on you." I almost growled out that statement. "Still, you're hiding something."

She pushed her tongue through my lips, kissing me as though she was trying to wash away the guilt. Whatever her reasons, I returned the kiss, needing to taste what was mine. And she was mine.

CHAPTER 2
LACEY

Coach Burton snapped his fingers. "Lacey, are you even listening? I thought you would be bouncing off the walls with this news that the Dodgers want to talk to you about a pitching position."

I flinched, tearing my attention away from the wall of photos behind Coach Burton's desk—pictures of teams he'd coached over the years.

I sucked in musty air and zeroed in on Coach's angular face. "When do the Dodgers want me in LA?" I should have been dizzy with excitement that my favorite baseball team wanted to talk to me—a female. Yet my voice held doom and gloom.

I was worried about Kade. Jen had been right. He'd looked pale. I suspected he had a migraine, and I'd probably made it worse. Kade despised when any guy touched me, even his own brothers. I couldn't say I blamed him for getting jealous. He didn't know Randy at all. I would have been acting the same if a girl I didn't know had been hugging on my man. But I owed Randy a huge thank-you. He'd found me sleepwalking across campus two nights ago.

9

Coach Burton scratched his head of brown hair and pinched his thick eyebrows. "You'll be getting a call from their front office with all the details."

I rose from the chair. "Thank you."

He glanced up at me from his messy desk. "What's going on? I've known you for four years. I know you want this opportunity more than any guy on the team."

I shuddered. "I really am excited. I just have something more pressing on my mind."

He pushed to his feet and circled his desk to stand in front of me. "Whatever it is, it's got to be bad for you to sweep this great news aside." His tone softened. "Is it your PTSD?"

When I'd first arrived on campus four years ago, I met with Coach Burton and told him my backstory, including my PTSD. My dad had recommended that I fill my baseball coach in on my disorder. That way, if something did happen, he could help me.

"No." It wasn't exactly a lie. But I didn't want to tell him I was deciding how to break the news to Kade that I'd been sleepwalking and having nightmares since I'd found out that my grandfather was up for parole next month. I was worried Kade would stress out and end up with severe migraines like he'd had back in high school when my grandfather had kidnapped me. Coach didn't need to know all those details. Besides, I had Kade there now to help me, and I was graduating tomorrow then moving home. "Kade isn't feeling well, and he's waiting for me." I headed for the door.

"Lacey, you have a great opportunity in front of you," Coach Burton said. "But make sure you have the support of your family. Otherwise, this journey will be extremely hard for you, especially since you could be the first female to be signed by a major league team. If that happens, the media will be all over you."

I went back to Coach and gave him a hug. "Thank you for everything." He'd been a confidant and like a dad to me.

He placed a large hand on my upper back as he walked me to the door. "Please let me know how the meeting goes with the Dodgers. I know you'll knock 'em dead."

My stomach revved up at how proud and excited he was for me. As I left his office, the news began to sink in. I could be the first female in the major leagues. I'd always dreamed of playing men's baseball. But if I was being honest with myself, I didn't think I would ever get an opportunity.

I couldn't get my hopes up. The Dodgers wanted to talk to me. I wasn't going to LA to sign a contract. Still, it was a step in the right direction, and for that, I smiled and practically skipped into town, which wasn't that far on foot.

The closer I got to the bed and breakfast, the more my smile waned. Kade wasn't going to let up about Randy. So I had to come clean. I wouldn't lie to him, but I also didn't want to conjure up the past or old demons, and my grandfather was a demon, at least in my book. Not to mention, when I told Kade about the sleepwalking, he would probably freak out. I loved him for who he was, flaws and all, and he had one flaw that was his own worst enemy—he constantly worried about me. When he worried, he got migraines to the point that he had landed in the ER one time back in high school.

As I approached the Cape-Cod-style home, my mood tanked. Not only did I have to tell him about my sleepwalking, but I had to tell him about my grandfather. Or maybe he already knew, which was why he'd been pale. I was certain, though, he knew nothing about my sleep-walking or nightmares, and I would have been lying if I said I wasn't frightened to tell him. The moment I told him, the past would come roaring back, and all that hard work I'd put in taming my PTSD over the years would be for nothing, especially if my grandfather was released on parole.

I plastered on a fake smile, waving at Lee, the gray-haired lady and owner of the bed and breakfast, as I started up the stairs.

"Is he in room two?" I asked, knowing he was. Kade always stayed in the same room that overlooked the lake, although it was much smaller than the lake behind Kade's home in Ashford.

"He is. Lacey?" She called my name with a hint of apprehension in her voice.

I grabbed onto the rail, stopping on the top step.

"Is something wrong with Kade? He doesn't look well." Her motherly concern was heartwarming and confirmed my suspicions that he had a migraine.

It didn't help that he'd seen Randy's arms around me.

I shrugged. "Not sure."

The phone on the counter next to her rang.

She reached for the receiver as I continued my quest down the hall. The doors to the rooms had simple locks with real keys and not the electronic keycards like the big hotels.

Kade never locked the door, especially if he knew I was coming. When I entered the room, I found him asleep. He had one hand underneath his pillow and the other tucked close to his chin. I hated to disturb him, so I slipped into bed and faced him, watching the way his chest slowly rose and fell.

The sun spilling in through the window behind him faded as I thought back to the first day I'd met the gorgeous man.

I jerked my head up. Some guy I didn't know stood behind my car. Panic set in. Since the police hadn't found the creeps who had invaded our home and murdered my mom and sister, I'd been extremely paranoid.

I opened my glove compartment, grasped the handle of my nine-millimeter handgun, then slowly got out. The stranger seemed frozen, staring at me as though he were contemplating his next move. I released a quiet breath, placing my free hand on the roof of my car and the other behind my back. Then I met his gaze. All sense of where I was vanished in that moment. The copper eyes staring back at me made my whole body quiver and my brain seize.

Between the sudden panic attacks that had become normal for me and trying hard to keep from blacking out, I was screwed.

Forget the tingles. My freaking belly had a thousand butterflies fluttering inside. I swallowed in order to get the saliva to coat my dry throat. Jeepers, I needed one of those five-gallon jugs of ice-cold Gatorade that a team usually threw over the winning coach.

After a few more swallows, I decided to give my voice a shot. The last thing I wanted to do was show fear. I was afraid that once I showed any sign of it, he would grab me with those muscular arms and drag me screaming into the nearby woods, where he would kill me the way they'd killed my sister and mom.

"You... have a problem?" I asked. I didn't think this guy was going to hurt me, but I couldn't be sure. Regardless, I had the gun in my hand, and I was committed.

"You need help?" the stranger asked as he stepped around the car toward me.

"I wouldn't come any farther," I warned. My fingers wound tightly around the handle of the gun. My muscles were tense enough to burst at any second.

"What are you doing out here all by yourself?" The guy stopped at the back edge of the car and turned his head left then right in quick succession.

The parking lot lights hit his face at just the right angle to illuminate his copper eyes with lashes so long that I shivered. Butterfly kisses. I imagined the light touch of those lashes skimming over my face or anywhere on my body. I didn't want to take my eyes off of him, but just that thought made my gaze wander slowly down his entire muscular body. His blue—or was it black?—T-shirt stretched tightly over his broad chest, emphasizing the word "Zeal" printed on the front. I didn't know if it was just a word he liked or if it was the band my father had signed. I continued my obvious assessment, holding the gun as steady as my trembling hand would allow, while my eyes landed on his faded worn jeans that hung low on his hips, tattered at the knees. "None of your business. What do you want?" I asked.

He took one step closer, and I whipped my hand around, aiming the gun at him.

He backed away, raising his hands to shoulder height, and as he did, his T-shirt lifted, exposing a small area just above his belt that made me suck in air.

Night turned to day as the feel of lips on mine made me moan.

When I blinked, Kade was fully awake—eyes open, tongue in my mouth, and an erection that caused me to moan even more.

All my problems became a distant memory as I mashed my body to his, feeling him, tasting him, and getting lost in us.

CHAPTER 3
KADE

I stripped her bare then shucked my clothes in a matter of seconds, wanting nothing more than to be inside of her, to feel every part of her as I shaped her curves. I slowly massaged her taut stomach, her ass, and her breasts before sucking and licking her from head to toe. Five years with this woman, and I still couldn't get enough of her. We'd had some great sex over the years, and it only seemed to get better and better.

She lay on her back, her long, wavy brown hair fanned out around her beautiful naked body, and her eyes full of love and lust. "Tell me, Kade, what you would like to do to me?" she asked in a breathy tone.

I chuckled softly as I sucked on her nipple, my dick grazing her inner thigh. "How many times do I have to tell you, showing is better than telling?" We had this same exchange of lines every time we were together. It was as though we'd written our own song—the prelude to our intimate dance.

She grabbed my rock-hard erection, or I should say Mr. Steel, as she liked to call my dick. My eyes rolled back in my head. At first, I thought she would guide me in, and I almost helped her along, desperately wanting to explode. Instead, I froze as we locked eyes.

"How about I tell you what I'm going to do to you?" Her sexy smile caused my dick to jerk in her hand.

"I'm all ears." The role reversal was new, and my body shuddered, eagerly awaiting her words.

Letting go of Mr. Steel, she sat up on her elbows.

I pouted.

She licked her lips. "I want you on your back while I suck on Mr. Steel until you're the one screaming my name."

I cocked an eyebrow, knowing I wouldn't last a second once she wrapped those thick lips of hers around my dick. As much as I wanted to fuck her until the sun set, I wanted her to do as she pleased. Seamlessly, we switched positions. Then she dragged her tongue down my chest, stopping to bite my nipples. The sensation only served to make me harder than the diamond that was tucked away in my jeans. My heart rate spiked and kept climbing the farther she traveled down my body. I thought of marriage, kids, and our future, and I almost blurted out "marry me," but then she would stop her assault, and her lips were so close to the tip of my dick.

She gazed up as though she were asking for permission.

I gently grabbed the sides of her head, my fingers getting lost in her hair. "Lace, if you don't act now, I will flip you over and fuck you hard."

Instantly, hunger flared in her eyes. "I want you to, but first..." She lowered her head and took me in her mouth.

When her tongue jumped into action, circling and licking, I let out a groan, then another until she sucked hard, and I shot up.

She giggled, no doubt loving the control she had over me.

Any migraine I'd had was gone. It also helped that I'd taken some medication as soon as I'd gotten back from her dorm. Stars coated my vision as I teetered on that blissful edge.

I pried her off me. "As much as I love your mouth on me, I want to be inside you."

Before I could flip her on her back, she scrambled quickly to straddle me. In one breath, she sank down on my dick, hard and fast. Then she stilled, sitting like a goddess, her breasts pushed out, her nipples taut, her hair messy about her face, and a frisky smile that said she was up to something.

Before I could blink, she squeezed, gripping my erection like a tightly worn glove.

Holy hell in water. Sweat broke out on my face as I recited to myself, "breathe, breathe, breathe." I had stamina, but the thread of resolve to hold out and enjoy watching her take control of my body was shredding fast. This wasn't the first time she'd teased me or made me sweat as I tried to hold back, but today seemed different. Maybe my feelings for her were heightened more than ever. The thought of having her home, in my bed, at my side, and as my partner for life was all-consuming, and I couldn't wait for us to start our lives together.

Flattening her hands on my chest, she lifted her hips up then down, pinning me with a sultry and satisfied look.

I flipped her and lost control.

I thrust into her, and we got into a rhythm as she matched my every move. Her hands were all over me, yet nowhere. I lowered my head until our mouths were fused, not breaking our stride.

The bed groaned, the headboard banged against the wall, she purred, and I grunted as the room and world around us disappeared. She arched into me, saying my name over and over until she shuddered. One last thrust, and I was falling into that blissful oblivion as I reached my release. Breathing heavily, I kissed her endlessly as I rode out my orgasm.

She wiped my hair from my forehead, her delicate fingers dancing down to my lips. "I love you, Kade Maxwell."

I couldn't help but grin as I rolled off her.

Blowing out a breath, she turned on her side and faced me. Her cheeks were flushed and glowing.

I picked strands of her hair from her sweat-sheened face. "So are you ready to tell me what's going on?"

She slipped her leg in between my thighs as her eyes clouded over. "Not really. I don't want you to get migraines or end up in the hospital like you did when we were in high school."

My heart stopped for a moment as I thought of what could have her spooked. "Baby, my migraines come and go whenever they want."

"But worry and stress don't help."

I kissed her nose. "We've been through hell and back, Lace. Whatever it is, I can handle it." My life had been a dark road since Karen's death, and the only light, aside from my family, was Lacey. She was the reason I was breathing.

She swallowed then worried her bottom lip. "I've been having nightmares again. Randy found me sleepwalking the other day, which was why I was hugging him. I wanted to thank him for finding me before I ended up..." She lowered her gaze.

I didn't want to think of what could've happened to her if Randy hadn't found her.

Fuck.

"Do you know why you're sleepwalking? Has this been happening the entire time you've been at college?" *Please tell me no.* I would kick myself repeatedly if I hadn't been with her to comfort and protect her.

She lifted her long lashes as a tear escaped. "My first year here was touch and go. I told you that. But I was also honest with you that I had my PTSD under control until I learned last week that my grandfather is up for parole a year earlier than expected." She puffed out her cheeks. "According to the LA newspaper, his lawyer appealed to the parole board, stating a model prisoner and good behavior. And since the prisons in California are overcrowded, he has a chance of getting out."

My migraine that had all but disappeared pricked at my temples.

Her grandfather, Harrison Lorenzino, Italian mob boss, had been convicted of being an accessory after the fact for her sister and mom's murders. He'd also been slapped with charges of kidnapping and attempted murder on Lacey. But before he'd gone to trial, his lawyers had cut a deal with the district attorney's office in California and with the federal government. In the end, the man had only been sentenced to ten years with the option for parole in six if he gave the FBI the information they wanted. And they wanted the locations of where all the money had been buried from a bank heist that Lacey's great-grandfather had been responsible for many years ago.

"If he does get parole, he can't leave the state of California. Besides, you and your dad don't have anything he wants anymore."

Apparently, James, Lacey's dad, had had a book that detailed some of the locations where the stolen money had been buried. At first, the FBI thought they had recovered all the money, but after all of it was counted, they realized they were still missing two million dollars. That was when the FBI had made the deal with Harrison.

"He scares me. I'm sorry I haven't told you sooner," she said. "I'd been hoping all of it would go away."

I interlocked our fingers. "Baby, I would kill the man if he so much as tried to come near you, and it's not like you'll be going anywhere near LA, anyway."

She stiffened. "The LA Dodgers want to talk to me about a pitching position." She feigned a smile.

Wow! She wasn't excited about maybe playing for a major league team? The despair in her voice broke my heart. The Dodgers was her favorite team. Her brother had played for them up until last year when he'd decided to hang up his hat and travel around the world.

I brushed my lips over hers. "Don't let the possibility of his parole ruin your dream, baby." As much as I wanted to start a family, I couldn't let her see or know the selfish reason why I wasn't jumping up and down for joy.

For the moment, I shucked the idea of proposing. No way did I want her to remember the proposal alongside her grandfather.

She dipped her chin as she looked away. "I'm super excited. But I'm scared to go to California."

Like hell would she go to California alone. The times of her wanting to do things on her own were over, especially when it came to her grandfather. "I'm going with you." Not to mention, California held so many memories for her that could trigger her PTSD at any time. After all, that was where her mom and sister had been murdered.

She gave me a half smile. "I need to do this alone."

I wasn't surprised at her answer. She'd said the same thing to me when she told me she would be going to Colby College. She'd needed to prove to herself that she could do things on her own. But living in Maine alone was vastly different than heading to a place that housed most of her triggers.

"Not this time, baby." I delivered the line with as much calmness as I could. "I know your independence is important to you. But for my own sanity, I can't let you go alone, and don't even tell me your brother, Rob, will be with you. Because last I heard, he's in Thailand." Her brother Rob had lived in LA up until he decided to travel around the world.

She sighed heavily. "Okay."

"Wow. No argument?"

She shrugged. "Maybe this is one time I need the big bad wolf with me."

I chuckled. "I'm not a bad wolf. Maybe a horny one."

She playfully swatted at me.

Then something hit me. If she did sign with the Dodgers, she would be living in California again. *Oh, man.* In only a few hours, our future had gone to shit. How could we live peacefully in the same state her grandfather resided in, the state that held such bad memories for her?

One day at a time my father had counseled on many occasions.

"I should hear from the Dodgers within the next week for more details," she said.

I rolled on my back, running a hand through my hair.

She climbed on top of me. "Do you realize that I might be the first female to enter the major leagues?" Her voice hitched, and a bright, sunny light shone in her eyes.

I rubbed the sides of her toned thighs. "You deserve the world, Lace."

She angled her head. "I detect a thread of unhappiness."

Busted.

I was serious when I said she deserved the world and more. All I'd ever wanted for her was to see her smiling every day and happy with life that didn't include PTSD, murder, kidnappings, and pain.

Yet I couldn't shake the idea of her living in California or us living in California. Not only that, if she signed a contract, would she still want to get married or have kids? Could she play pregnant? Again, I was getting too far ahead of myself.

One day at a time was becoming my mantra.

I grinned, albeit weakly. "I want a family, a big one. You know that. I don't want to wait much longer for us to settle down."

She smoothed a finger over my eyebrow. "We can get married in a couple of years once I get in the groove with my career. We love each other. So why rush into things?"

I moved her off me then got out of bed. When I did, the room spun. I staggered and caught the chair near the window.

Lacey was at my side in a flash. "What's wrong? It's a headache, isn't it? That's why you were sleeping when I came in. That's why you looked pale. Jennifer said that, and so did Lee at the front desk."

The room blurred. I wobbled to the chair and dropped my body into it. "I'm good. I just got up too quickly," I lied.

She didn't need another thing to worry about.

CHAPTER 4
LACEY

I clutched my stomach as I sat in a waiting room at the Dodgers' front office in Los Angeles. The past few weeks had been tumultuous with graduating, moving back home, losing sleep over my grandfather's parole hearing, and the excitement that a major league team was interested in me.

For the last twenty minutes, I'd been trying to rid myself of the nausea that had hit me all of a sudden. I blew out a breath, then another, and yet another. My nerves had been all over the place leading up to this exciting moment, but not to the point of wanting to puke my guts out.

I touched my forehead. No fever, but a light sheen of sweat coated my skin. It felt as though I'd just woken up from one of my bad dreams in which my grandfather was chasing me with a knife in his hand. That nightmare had been a staple of mine since I'd learned he could get out on parole. His hearing was scheduled for next week.

I wouldn't be able to sleep until after his hearing. I was certain Kade wouldn't, either. He'd been with me almost every night, comforting me when I jolted up from a nightmare crying and scream ing. I hated to see the pain on his face. I hated that we were reliving scenes from our high school senior year when he was constantly getting migraines and I was a hot mess with blackouts, nightmares, and panic attacks.

I tapped my foot as I glanced around the small waiting room that had pictures of baseball players, old and new, hanging on the walls. When my eyes landed on the jar of M&M's on the table beside me, bile rose. What in the world? I loved the chocolate candy.

The door to the conference room opened, and with it, a whoosh of cologne-infused air hit me square in the nose. Covering my mouth with my hand, I jumped up. Not the reaction I was going for when meeting the Dodgers management team.

A petite lady with kind brown eyes rushed forward. "Ms. Robinson, you look extremely pale." She rested her hand on my back. "The restroom is around the corner on your right. Why don't you give yourself a minute to freshen up? I'll let them know you'll be right in."

I inhaled another whiff of that musky cologne. Immediately, a macabre memory flitted through my head. I pushed that dark night away—the night I'd come home to find the dead bodies of my mom and sister. Maybe being in LA was causing me to be sick. After all, I grew up there. My sister and mom were murdered there, and my grandfather resided in a California prison. I didn't care to know which one.

Kade should've come to the meeting with me instead of hanging at the hotel. He had insisted, but I'd wanted to at least attend the meeting on my own. As much as I loved him, I couldn't have him holding my hand every waking minute. This was my career, and if I were going to play in the major leagues, then I had to be strong. I had to lift up my chin, roll back my shoulders, and swallow my nausea.

Regardless, I should at least splash water on my face then pinch my cheeks to get color back. I couldn't let them see me sweat, especially for the wrong reasons. They might think I was petrified of them and the opportunity, and while I was a little, I believed my paleness was a direct result of nerves and stress, or maybe I was getting the flu. I did feel as if someone had zapped the energy out of me.

I stuck out my chest. I definitely had to bite the bullet and walk into that room even if I was about to puke or collapse. Because if I ran to the bathroom, they would think I wasn't cut out for the team. After all, any man in my shoes, no matter how he was feeling, would appear strong on the outside.

"I'm good." *Not in the least.*

Maybe I had food poisoning from that hamburger I ate last night, or maybe the eggs on the plane that morning weren't agreeing with my stomach. *Or maybe you're still spooked over your grandfather's parole.* Which according to my dad wouldn't happen. He'd said the district attorney in LA believed that my grandfather wouldn't be paroled early. There were too many others in the prison system with lesser crimes who qualified for early parole.

She dipped her bright-red head. "Very well. By the way, I'm Holly, Brice Thames's assistant. We spoke on the phone." She waved me in.

As soon as I walked into the conference room, acid crept up to my throat. As gross as it was, I smiled through a swallow at the three men who rose from their leather chairs.

I ambled over to one of two empty seats. Holly was right beside me until she slid into the chair in front of her laptop, next to the bald man I knew as Tony Greer. He was the scout who'd been to several of my games over the last year.

"Lacey, nice to see you again," Tony said. "Please have a seat."

I nodded as I took the one remaining spot at the head of the table.

Holly made the introductions.

The black man to my right was Brice, who led the Dodgers' Triple-A division, and the large man across from Brice was Marcel Lentz, president of the scouting division.

I clasped my hands together on the table, trying not to inhale the strong scent of cologne.

Holly started. "The team will ask you a series of questions. Once you've answered them, then you can ask a few of your own. Afterward, we'll adjourn, and the team will collaborate."

The three men opened their notebooks.

Marcel ran a hand down his Dodgers tie and over his large stomach. "So Lacey, we've seen your tapes. I have to say I was a bit shocked that a petite woman like you can throw a fastball at almost ninety miles an hour. Can you talk to us about your workout regimen?" His skepticism rang out loud and clear.

I knew I would have to sell myself, and to a certain extent, my skills, although the tapes of my games spoke for themselves. Facts didn't hide anything.

I sat up straighter, despite my sickness. "During my college years, I've been working out in the weight room three days a week in the off-season and every day during the season when I didn't have a game. On top of that, I practice my pitching year-round." I'd been relentless in getting back into the game after the funeral six years ago, but even more so when I entered college. My time in the weight room certainly showed on my arms, chest, and legs. I wasn't big by any means, but I was strong.

Holly typed on her laptop, while the others jotted notes in their books.

Brice piped in next, settling his stark green gaze on me. "We like what we saw on your tapes. Tony also tells us that the crowd loves you. How do you handle the media? And were the men on your college team receptive to you?"

Coach Burton had said the media would have a field day with me if I signed a major league contract. But the local media, and at times the national media, had been at my college games. So I was used to answering reporters' questions.

I smiled at Brice. "I'm not sure what you're looking for, but I'm very cordial and professional when speaking with the media. As far as the men on the team, we got along great." That was the truth. My teammates hadn't given me any problems like Aaron Seever had back in high school.

Brice jotted something in his notebook, giving me no indication if he liked my answer or not. Frankly, I couldn't worry about what he thought. I'd been honest.

They asked me several more questions: Do you have an agent? Are you prepared for the media frenzy? How will you focus when the world will be watching a woman pitch in the major leagues? How will you deal with the men on the team who believe that a woman shouldn't be playing a man's game?

I answered the questions as best I could. None of them gave away what they were thinking about my answers. When it was my turn to ask questions, I really had only one for the men.

"How do you men feel about a woman on the team?" I asked.

Given Brice's question about how receptive the men had been when I joined my college team, I had a feeling he wasn't all that enamored with a woman on his team.

The three men honed in on me as fast as a whip. Holly, on the other hand, smiled.

The nausea in my stomach dulled.

Brice's green eyes seemed to glow against his dark skin. He reminded me of a cross between Derek Jeter and Alex Rodriguez. Handsome for sure. "To be frank, having a woman on the team would be a challenge for this organization. I don't think we're quite ready for that."

My intuition had been spot-on.

"Brice," Marcel said. "Whether or not we're ready, Lacey is that good. Let's not forget you need a closer on the team. With Freddy's arm shot, you've lost the last three games. So when we return after the All-Star break, what are you going to do?"

I sucked in a quiet breath. I had one person in my court. Actually two. Tony Greer had scouted me, which meant that he'd pushed to set up this meeting.

Tony pointed his pen at Brice. "We've discussed this. Whether the men want a woman on the team or not, she's got the talent. If anyone on the team has a stick up their ass over her, then she'll deal with it, and I'm sure you will help her as well. That is if you want to win games."

My head swung from right to left as the men continued to argue. Holly winked at me. I imagined she heard all kinds of arguments.

I sat up straighter. "Mr. Thames, I understand some of your concerns. But as Mr. Greer has pointed out, my stats speak volumes. The question is do you want to take a chance on me? Does the Dodgers organization want to take a chance on signing the first female to their roster?" *Please say yes.* "I've dealt with boys not wanting a girl on the team, but in the end, their reason has been they were afraid I would take away the spotlight from them. They were worried I would show them up. But baseball is a team game. It takes all nine players to win a game. I, for one, am a team player." I wanted to say *regardless if I peed standing up or sitting down, I could play the game.*

Brice mashed his lips together in response, nodding. He was a hard man to read.

"Lacey, do you have any other questions for them?" Holly asked.

I had two. "When will you make your decision, and when you do, what are the next steps?"

Coach Burton had called me last week to give me some last-minute advice on making sure I knew where I stood before I left the meeting.

Tony cleared his throat. "Give us a couple of days."

Marcel clasped his hands on his large belly. "Why don't we see Lacey in action while she's in LA? We have a handful of ball players in town despite the All-Star break. Let's call them in to work out with her."

Brice raised a thick brow. "Great idea."

My mouth parted.

Tony rose. "It's settled. Can you meet us at the stadium at nine a.m. tomorrow?"

27

Thankfully, I had packed my cleats and glove. Holly hadn't mentioned that they would have me pitch, but my dad had said to be prepared just in case. "Of course." Kade and I weren't flying home for another two days. I wanted to visit Julie and Mom's grave, and I could do that later in the day.

We shook hands before Holly walked me out.

"You did well in there," she said. "I hope you feel better by the morning."

I pushed the button on the elevator. "It was touch and go, but suddenly the wave of nausea is gone."

She angled her head. "Is this nausea happening every day?"

"No. I think I was extremely nervous."

The elevator doors opened.

"Mm," she said. "Well, give them hell tomorrow."

I stepped into the empty car. "I plan to."

The doors slid shut, and I squealed. I couldn't wait to tell Kade. More importantly, I couldn't wait to show Brice Thames that a woman could handle the men and the game.

CHAPTER 5
KADE

Lacey tossed and turned, keeping me awake for the last two hours. I hadn't slept a full night since she moved back home. Her nightmares kept me on edge and holding her into the wee hours of the morning. I couldn't believe how years of improvement had been washed away with one news report.

I let out a sigh, knowing she wasn't screaming at the moment, nor was she crying or talking in her sleep as she usually did when she was freaked out about something. I was certain that her chance to show the LA Dodgers how great a pitcher she was helped to keep the subject of her grandfather at bay.

As for me, I wanted to get on the next plane out of LA. Home was not here, and if the Dodgers did sign her, then I wasn't sure what I would do. Shortly after her sister and mom's funeral, her psychiatrist had recommended a change of scenery, which had helped Lacey tremendously. If she returned to LA, I wasn't sure she would ever heal.

One day at a time. I'd been trying to follow that advice, but it was hard as fuck when all I kept envisioning was a future where neither Lacey nor me were happy.

29

The ring of her phone blasted through the quietness of the hotel room. I bolted out of bed and grabbed it from the nightstand on the other side of Lacey.

"Hey, James," I whispered, walking away. "What's wrong?" He wouldn't have woken us up at six in the morning if something weren't wrong, although it was nine a.m. back home.

"Sorry to wake you," he said. "I got a call from the LA DA. He thinks it would be good to have Lacey testify against Harrison's release at the parole hearing. I told him no, but he wants to talk with Lacey."

I glanced at my girl, who was curled into a fetal position, finally not moving as she slept soundly.

I quietly grabbed a room key and stepped out into the hall. "Are you kidding me?" I tried to keep my voice low as I trudged by rooms on my way to the small alcove of elevators. "I can't let her do that. Do you know she's been dreaming of Harrison killing her? Testifying will only make her PTSD even worse than it is now. In fact, if you think she was out of control in high school, you haven't seen anything yet." I didn't know if Lacey had told her old man about her sleepwalking, but he had to know. "She's even sleepwalking."

He sucked in a sharp breath. "Fuck."

"Yeah, fuck. But she has a tryout today, which she's extremely excited about. So I'm not saying anything about talking to the DA, at least not until she's finished with her tryout. Besides, didn't the LA DA cut Harrison a deal?"

"He's a newly appointed DA. The other one retired."

Harrison probably had the retired DA on his mob's payroll.

My mind was on high alert. "How does he even know Lacey is in town?"

"He didn't. He called me, and I told him he might be able to meet her to chat before she left LA. Look, I'll text you the DA's info. Talk to Lacey. I got a meeting to get to." Then he hung up.

I wanted to throw her phone through the window and into the fog that hung over the city.

30

I growled as my brain worked overtime. *Pack up and get out.* If I knew it wouldn't cause a fight between Lacey and me or ruin her chance to play baseball, I would whisk her away faster than the speed of light to a place that didn't have news reporters, baseball, or anything that could set off her panic attacks. But I was living in a fairy tale.

"Ha," I said out loud. "Fairy tales have their own problems, enemies, and demons." I laughed when a businessman dressed in a sharp striped suit strutted up to the elevators.

He stabbed the down button, giving me a once-over.

It took me a second to realize I'd walked out in my underwear.

"Rough night," I said as I casually made my way back to the room, not giving a shit about how I looked.

When I waved the keycard in front of the metal panel above the doorknob, a pain gripped the back of my head. Then a dull throbbing began and so did the onset of a migraine. I hadn't had a headache since I was in Maine for Lacey's graduation. Which wasn't that odd considering my headaches weren't on a time schedule.

Once inside, I glanced at Lacey, who was still curled up, sleeping soundly.

As quietly as I could, I found my bag and popped some Advil before starting a pot of coffee.

When the machine started gurgling, Lacey stirred before she opened her eyes. "Morning."

My groin reacted to her sultry voice. We'd had more sex in the last several weeks than we'd had all of last year, and boy, what a ride it had been. Maybe that was one of the reasons I hadn't had a headache, although now that I thought about it, we didn't have sex last night. She'd been so tired that she'd fallen asleep as soon as we returned from dinner. Plus, the time change didn't help.

Suddenly, all thought disappeared as I laid eyes on her naked breasts. As she sat up, her messy hair fell forward before she cleared it from her face.

I pounced, and in a flash, I had her on her back, hovering over her.

She giggled. "One night without sex, and you're a madman. I wonder what you did when I was away at college."

I cocked an eyebrow. "Seriously? How many times did we have phone sex?" Man, those calls had been the bomb. I would tell her what I would do to her, and she would moan and moan until her release while I jacked off.

She rubbed herself against me. "Did I hear my phone ring earlier?"

I sucked on a nipple. "You want to talk about a ringing phone?"

She latched on to my dick. "No."

When she spewed that word, I tore off my boxer briefs and buried myself inside her. She arched into me, and I nibbled and sucked anywhere on her body I could reach until we were both groaning in pure unadulterated pleasure.

Three hours later, after another heart-pumping lovemaking session, we were at Dodger Stadium. I wasn't a huge baseball fan, at least not a Dodgers fan. But I couldn't help the awe that rippled through me as I stood on the field, even more so as I watched Lacey throw pitch after pitch. Her slider was spot-on. Her curveball was a little shaky, but her fastball topped all of her pitches.

The African-American man standing behind the catcher pointed a radar gun, clocking Lacey's pitches. Lacey had informed me that Brice Thames was the one who was skeptical of a woman on his Triple-A team. However, the awe on his face as the ball thudded into the catcher's mitt might change his mind.

Their scout, Tony Greer, who lingered next to Brice, shouted out, "Ninety-two. Well done, Lacey."

The handful of players scattered around exchanged shocked looks.

My phone vibrated against my leg. I dipped into the pocket of my jeans and pulled it out. "Hey, James."

"Did you get my text? Have you had a chance to talk to Lacey? The DA is wanting to meet with her today."

"She's right in the middle of showing the Dodgers what she's made of. So, no. I don't plan on it, either. I thought about it." Hell, that was all I'd kept thinking about on our way to the stadium. "She doesn't need to get involved with Harrison's case."

"I don't like this any better than you. But if her testimony can keep my old man in jail another year, then I'll take that." He huffed out a grunt. "Have you proposed yet?"

A wave of confusion crossed over me at how he bounced from one subject to the other. I walked along the first baseline toward right field. "Boy, that came out of nowhere. I haven't. She's distracted, and I want her full attention."

I'd asked him for her hand in marriage over three months ago. He was elated that I was finally going to pop the question. Other than him, my father and my best friend, Hunt, knew too. I was careful to keep the news to only those individuals. If I told my brothers, I was afraid word would leak to their girlfriends, then Lacey would find out.

"Kade," James said. "Are you backing out of the proposal?"

I threaded my fingers through my hair. "You didn't call me to talk about the proposal." As I turned around to watch Lacey, my heart stopped. "Fuck." I ran toward the mound. Flashes of the past played before me in slow motion. The first time Lacey tried out for the high school baseball team, she'd blacked out and fallen face-first in the middle of a pitch.

"What's wrong?" James asked in a panicked voice.

"Lacey is throwing up. I'll call you back."

The players around her stayed in their positions almost looking dumbfounded.

I squatted down, thankful at least that she wasn't out cold.

She heaved up her breakfast once more before wiping her mouth with the back of her hand. Blowing a breath, she closed her eyes for a second before she hopped to her feet, rolled her shoulders back, and eyed Brice. "I'm fine."

She didn't look fine.

Brice didn't say a word as he continued to fixate on Lacey.

Tony Greer, who stood next to Brice, had concern written all over his face. Hell, I had to have the same look. I'd seen Lacey black out, have nightmares, and experience panic attacks, but I'd never seen her get sick.

I laid a hand on her back. "Are you sure you're okay?"

She batted her long lashes at me. "Never better."

Liar.

I wasn't about to say that out loud, though. I knew she was trying to prove to these men that a woman could cut it in the big leagues, although her puking in front of the people she had to convince probably wasn't boding well for her. For that reason, my heart sank to the mound.

Finally, Brice spoke. "I've seen enough." He raised his voice, regarding the players. "Thanks, guys, for helping out today."

They converged in the dugout. Tony left Brice's side to chat with one of the players.

With a white-as-snow face, Lacey tucked her glove underneath her arm and sashayed up to Brice. "Did I convince you?" Her tone was a little shaky.

Brice raked his gaze over her. "We can't have you puking on the mound in a game. I get the nerves, but I—"

"I'm sorry about that," Lacey said. "I think I have the flu or ate bad food." Her tone was even.

Brice removed his Dodgers hat, swiped a hand over his head, then placed the hat back on. "We'll be in touch." He collected his bag before leaving the field.

I had the urge to call him a rude ass. Instead I bit my tongue as I sidled up to Lacey. I wasn't there to get in the middle of her career. I was there to support her, and mouthing off to her potential manager wouldn't have done her any good, although it would have made me feel better.

Lacey dropped her head back, glancing up at the clear blue sky. When she righted her head, she grabbed her stomach.

The catcher, a somewhat tall guy, broad in the shoulders and wearing an easy smile, moseyed over. "If it's any consolation, I was nervous the day I had to prove myself. You're good, Lacey Robinson." He turned to Tony Greer behind him. "She belongs on the team."

Tony scratched the top of his bald head. "I know that. Right now it's Brice's call. Upper management is leaving the decision to him."

Lacey flicked off her ball cap. "Please look past my sickness," she said to Tony. "You know I can do this. You've watched me for the last two years."

He gave her a weak smile. "I know you can play. Again, it's not up to me."

The catcher said to Lacey, "I hope to see you again." He jogged off with the rest of the players.

"Thanks for your help today," Lacey shouted. No sooner had she said the last word than she covered her mouth with her hand and bolted off the field through the dugout.

I was about to follow, when Tony held out his hand. "Kade, can I ask you a personal question? You don't have to give me an answer. In fact, I could lose my job by asking with all the discrimination laws in this country. But I don't care. I believe in Lacey and her talent. After Lacey left the meeting yesterday, Holly, Brice's assistant, mentioned to me that she thought Lacey might be pregnant. Is that true?"

I choked. "Come again?" Lacey pregnant? That couldn't be. She was on the pill and had been since I met her. "Did Lacey tell Holly that?"

He mashed his lips into a thin line. "Not really. Call it a woman's intuition, although with Lacey throwing up, maybe Holly's right." He twisted his wedding band around on his finger. "With the Pregnancy Discrimination Act, we can't use her pregnancy as a reason not to sign her, although I suspect a doctor would recommend that she couldn't play after six or eight weeks into her pregnancy. Still, we have more than six weeks of games coming up."

The empty blue seats spun before me. Blackness crept into my peripheral vision. So many things ran rampant through my mind. If she were pregnant, then she wouldn't play baseball, which meant she wouldn't be traveling. Then we could get married and settle down sooner like I wanted to. *Selfish ass.* Regardless, I wanted to shout to the vacant stadium that I was going to be a dad—something I'd been dreaming about since I met Lacey. Okay, well not the minute I met her, but I'd always imagined how our kids would look.

My niece, Raven, looked exactly like my mom with black hair and blue eyes. Actually, she resembled my triplet brothers, especially her father, Kross. I pictured my child having Lacey's luscious green eyes and wavy brown hair, maybe even a head full of curls whether we had a boy or a girl.

Tony snapped his long fingers. "Kade, are you okay?"

Hell no.

My mind waged a war. Lacey wouldn't be happy if she were pregnant, and even though I would be over the fucking moon, we both had to want a child. That was how a relationship worked.

Tony clutched my arm. "It could very well be the flu or bad food like Lacey said."

I chuckled, the act calming me for the moment.

Tony lowered his gaze to his watch. "We have a meeting to discuss Lacey."

"Who else knows about this besides you and Holly?" If Brice knew, he would definitely not give her a shot.

He dipped his head. "Just Holly and me. Again, it's all speculation on Holly's part. She is rooting for Lacey too. But after her throwing up on the mound—"

"She's not pregnant," I blurted out.

He arched an eyebrow. "The shock on your face tells me you really don't know the answer. Look, this speculation isn't going to change my vote. However, regardless if she is or isn't, she can't be throwing up in a game. I know that is now a concern of Brice's. I'm going to be late." He sauntered off and up the steps behind home plate.

I went in search of my girl, thinking of Lacey pregnant. Man, I wanted her to be more than anything in this world. But I also wanted her to be happy, and that meant playing baseball, whether it was with the Dodgers or not.

My heart rate sped up as I entered the ladies' restroom not far from the men's locker room, even more so when I heard Lacey crying. I kicked my legs into gear as I turned a corner, passing the stalls and heading into an open area where I found her bent over one of five sinks, puking and crying at the same time.

I smoothed a hand over her sweaty hair. Then I kissed her head.

She simpered as she locked eyes with me in the mirror. "You're a brave man for coming near me while I'm losing my breakfast and last night's dinner."

I moved over to lean against the counter. "I love you, puke and all."

A tear slid down her face. "I can't believe I puked out on the mound. They'll never sign me now."

I caught the tear before it dropped on her T-shirt. "It happens."

She laughed nervously. "A guy wouldn't puke."

I touched her forehead much like my mom had done when she thought us boys had been sick as kids. "You don't know that." She didn't feel as though she had a fever. "So do you think you're sick from bad food?"

She shrugged. "I started feeling icky while I was waiting for the meeting yesterday. It's just nerves."

She could be right. "So according to Tony, Brice's assistant thinks you're pregnant."

A deep crease formed between her eyebrows. "I'm not. I'm on the pill." Then her eyes glazed over, no doubt thinking hard.

For several seconds, we stared at each other until the trilling sound of my phone ringing severed our connection. "James."

Lacey splashed water on her face.

"She's okay," I said in lieu of hello.

She snagged a paper towel then grabbed the phone from me. "I'm fine, Dad. Yeah. I'll call you later." She handed the phone back to me. "He wants to talk to you."

No doubt. But the LA DA could wait. I had something far more important to discuss with my girl. I walked around the corner to where the stalls were so there wouldn't be a chance Lacey could hear her father.

"Call the DA," James said. "Do it now." His tone permitted no argument.

I wanted to reach through the phone and strangle James on his insistency over the DA. "I'll handle it," I bit out before I ended the call. I was certain Lacey heard me snap at her father.

When I cleared the corner, she was patting her face with a paper towel. "You and my dad fighting?"

"The DA in LA wants to talk to you about your grandfather's parole hearing."

She chewed on her lip, staring at herself in the mirror.

I gripped the sides of her arms from behind. "You don't have to do this."

She twirled around so we were facing each other. "Maybe I am pregnant."

I could feel my eyebrows coming together. "Did you hear what I said about the parole hearing?"

"What if I am pregnant," she said more than asked. She touched her stomach. "Oh my God. I wouldn't be able to play baseball." Panic coated every word.

I literally scratched my head as I edged back. I shouldn't have been surprised or hurt at her shock and disappointment, but I was. I wanted to say, "What about marriage? What about starting a family?" But relationships were give and take. Still, I was ready to combust. I was ready to tie her down so she couldn't leave me again. Selfish or not, I shouldn't beat myself up for wanting to start a life with the woman I love—the same woman who had such a strong fucking hold on my

38

heart that I now understood why Kelton had always been so closed off to love. "Women break your heart," he'd said.

Lacey placed a soft hand on my rough jaw. "Hey, are you in there? Did you hear me?"

Loud and clear.

As though she knew what I was thinking, she said, "I know we've been apart a long time, but if they offer me a contract, I can't pass that up." She was almost in tears.

Ah, hell. I would never tell her not to go. As much as I wanted her to stay, I loved her too much to take away her dream. She would always resent me too.

She locked her hands around my neck; her acid breath was almost dragon fire. "I love the crap out of you, Kade Maxwell. I just can't be pregnant right now. No team would sign me if I was carrying a baby. They might not even like it if I get married."

Well, there went that proposal. Heat gripped my cheeks like a vise. "Why would they protest if we got married?"

She let go of me. "They would think if I was married, then a baby would be next. As a female, I don't have it as easy as a man would have."

My nostrils flared even though I knew she was right. "According to Tony, they won't know if you're pregnant unless you tell them. He said something about discrimination laws and a pregnancy discrimination act."

She lifted a shoulder. "It probably doesn't matter now. If they suspect I'm pregnant, then they won't even consider me." Tears flowed down her rosy cheeks. "They'll probably come up with some excuse other than pregnancy."

I tipped up her chin. "Tony and Holly are rooting for you. I am too."

Her hands slid up my chest. Her touch electrified and centered me even though I swayed to one side.

She tapped my face. "Are you all right? You're the one now who looks white as a ghost."

Maybe I had vertigo, and that was the reason for my dizziness lately.

I shuddered. "I can't breathe without you." I cupped her gorgeous face. "But I want you to have the world."

She gave me an award-winning smile. "Regardless of what the Dodgers decide, I would be ecstatic if I were carrying your child."

Man, a wave of relief settled over me. "Our child. First, we should find out if you're pregnant."

For the longest moment, she gave me a contemplative look. "My period is due next week. So let's wait on that." She lifted up on her tiptoes and kissed me. Then she giggled. "I'm sorry. My breath is nasty."

I tapped her on the nose. "It is, but I would kiss you, anyway."

"Let's go back to the hotel," she said. "I need mouthwash and a nap. I feel like someone sucked the wind out of me."

I rubbed her neck. "What about the DA?"

"Can we talk to him later this afternoon after I visit Julie's and Mom's graves?"

If it were up to me, I would say no. But maybe trying to help keep her grandfather behind bars would help tame Lacey's PTSD.

CHAPTER 6
LACEY

The balmy LA weather enveloped me as I sat on the grass, staring at the headstones of my sister and my mom. When they were first buried, I would sit for hours and hours, even falling asleep right in this very spot. It had been years since I'd been there. For some odd reason, the cemetery gave me a sense of peace. I plucked a blade of grass, then another, thinking back on my life since their deaths.

I wished I was totally healed from my PTSD, but Dr. Davis had said that I would probably never be rid of the symptoms or the memories or flashbacks. I'd done a good job while in college with the occasional panic attack that didn't affect my everyday life like it had in high school. But with the news of my grandfather's parole, all bets were off the table.

The nightmares were coming in full force. Heck, I had even sleep-walked for the first time since their funeral. Maybe it was best if I did testify against my grandfather's parole. I'd never gotten the chance to get up on the stand when he was on trial all those years ago. The government didn't need me then. My father's testimony had been enough along with other indisputable facts of the case.

Regardless, I wanted to whisper out loud to Julie and Mom and tell them that my future was bright and sunny and full of great things. I couldn't. If my grandfather got out of jail, I was afraid I wouldn't have a future. PTSD would certainly rule my life.

I wasn't there to relive that dreadful night when I'd walked into the house and found blood everywhere along with Julie and Mom dead. So I shifted to all the good times Julie, Mom, and I had had. I thought about how we'd had spa days and shopping sprees and had even sat around the fireplace just chatting about nothing. I smiled as I touched my stomach. Maybe being pregnant would be good. I wanted to have at least one or two girls. Kade and I had always agreed that it didn't matter what the sex of our babies were, as long as they were healthy. But as I read Julie's epitaph, the girl who brightened a room, I wanted a girl more than anything just to name her Julie. If I had two girls, I would definitely name the other one Laura, after my mom.

I lost my smile. "I wish you were both here with me. I wish I could see your faces when you met Kade for the first time or his brothers, even his parents. You would love Kade's mom. Dad misses you both so much, as do I. I know Rob does too. I know you're looking down on me. I know you're protecting me. So if you can hear me, tell those angels above to make sure my grandfather doesn't get parole."

A light wind blew, and with it, Kade's woodsy scent tickled my nose. When we'd gotten to the cemetery, Kade hung back at the rental car, talking to the DA. He'd also wanted to give me some alone time with Julie and Mom. I tossed a look over my shoulder and found him with sadness written all over his face. I suspected he'd heard me. More than that, I suspected he was thinking about his own sister, Karen.

The Maxwells had had their fair share of death and heartbreak.

"Karen would've loved you," Kade said as he helped me to my feet.

A chill crawled down my back. "Don't ever leave me."

His arms went around me. "Hey, I'm not going anywhere."

"You don't know what fate has in store for us, and I don't want to be talking to your gravestone."

He rubbed my back. "Baby, stop thinking morbid thoughts."

I nuzzled into his hard chest, absorbing his manly scent, breathing a sigh of relief, knowing he loved me. The first year of college without him at my side had been scary, death-defying, lonely, and I'd found it hard to breathe. I had cried most nights in my dorm, barely keeping my mind focused on classes, always wondering when my PTSD might hit me or when one of my triggers would surface. For example, a dark house or dark building would send me spiraling into a blackout. But I believed all the worrying I did that first year had helped me become more aware of my triggers, which was one of the reasons I'd kept my PTSD mostly at bay.

"What's going on in that beautiful head of yours?" Kade's husky voice shattered all those memories of loneliness in college and sleepless nights without him.

I craned my neck. "I was thinking how much I love you."

He lowered his head, ghosting his lips over mine. "Baby, you're the best thing that has ever happened to me." He kissed me, slow and tentative.

That chill I'd had a moment ago was replaced by tingles that coated my body as I pushed my tongue into his mouth. He tasted of happiness and sunshine. He'd always taken away the bad memories. He'd always been there to catch me when I fell. He'd been the guy who didn't run when he'd seen me black out or have one of my panic attacks. He'd been the man who held me when I had nightmares.

He had the biggest heart of anyone I knew. He kissed me wildly as his strong hands got lost in my hair. I wanted to stay right in that spot and kiss him forever. But forever died when my phone broke the veil of silence that surrounded us.

He groaned as he always did when someone or something interrupted us.

I dipped into my purse and removed my phone. My eyes went wide when I recognized the number. "It's the Dodgers."

The ringing continued as I fumbled with the phone, almost dropping it. "Hello." My voice shook.

"Lacey, this is Brice Thames. Are you feeling better?"

"Yes, sir." I'd taken a nap and had a handful of crackers earlier. Still, my nerves spiked high, waiting for him to continue.

"Good to hear," he said. "We just got out of our meeting, and we'd like for you to join us next week in Oklahoma and practice with the team."

I held my bottom lip hostage. "So no contract?"

"I want you to meet the team and practice with them. If all goes well, then we can talk contract."

I couldn't say I wasn't disappointed because I was. Then again, given that Tony and Holly suspected I was pregnant, I was also surprised I still had an opportunity to convince Brice I was the right person for the job. Although maybe he was taking things slow in the event I was pregnant. That way, he wouldn't have to go through signing me and getting the fans and media all excited about signing a girl only to have to dissolve the contract when I had to stop playing, which might not go over well with the Dodgers or the fans.

"With Freddie out, I thought you needed a pitcher to start after the All-Star break."

"You let me worry about that. So are you in?"

I glanced up at Kade. "Can I call you back in an hour? I want to talk it over with my boyfriend." It was as much my decision as it was Kade's. I'd learned from my mom that major decisions should be discussed with your significant other.

"I'll expect to hear from you in an hour," he said. Then the phone line went dead.

I widened my eyes. I couldn't believe I hadn't said yes.

"I heard most of the conversation," Kade said. "So why do you have to get my opinion?"

44

I poked him in the chest. "Because that's what couples do. We talk about things."

He brought my hand up to his mouth "You can't pass this up." He kissed my palm. "This could lead to a contract."

I bit my lip. "I know. But with the idea of me being pregnant—"

He placed a finger on my mouth. "You said yourself your period isn't due until next week. There's no harm in practicing with the team. Brice is feeling you out. It's all part of the interview process. And if it turns out you're pregnant, we'll cross that bridge then."

Even though he was right, I should say no, maybe because Kade was wincing.

"Is it a headache?" I asked.

A hard wind blew, causing some strands of his hair to fall in his eyes. After he flicked away his hair, he painted on one of his famous blank expressions that I hated. He wasn't telling me something.

"No," he said emphatically. "We should go. With traffic, I don't want to be late for our meeting with Mr. Brandt."

I huffed out a sigh, debating whether to push him for a straight answer. I chose not to. I didn't want to get into an argument in the middle of the cemetery, especially not with an old man walking toward us, holding flowers.

My heart tripped a beat at the sadness written all over the old man's face. I had the urge to console him. On that thought, I walked up to him. "Sir, I'm so sorry for your loss."

He stopped dead in his tracks and regarded me with a nod of his head. "Thank you." Then he took one of my hands in his. "Death is never easy." He glanced at Kade. "Make sure you put your loved ones before anything else." He sounded as though he were guilty of not taking his own advice.

I checked on Kade, who was rubbing one of his temples. When I turned back to the old man, he was gone. I spotted him two rows down, setting the flowers on the ledge of a gravestone. I watched him bless himself before I joined Kade.

"Are you one hundred percent sure you're okay? I mean physically?" I swallowed hard as an eerie feeling careened through me. I shivered despite the warm sunshine.

He kissed me on the head. "I am."

I didn't believe him. But I learned long ago that pushing Kade for an answer was futile. When he was ready, he would tell me.

For now, we made our way to the rental car in silence.

Within thirty minutes, we were sitting in the lobby of the hotel, surrounded by light music, people coming and going, and others sitting in chairs, absorbed in their phones or on their computers. Every now and then, the fragrant aroma of orchids floated our way from the large vase of flowers sitting on a table near the entrance.

"I texted the DA and told him where we were in the hotel," Kade said.

I stared at the bar area across from us. I'd had one or two beers throughout my college years, but I'd never gotten drunk or drank until I was feeling buzzed like most of the kids at frat parties had. My baseball coach would've had my head on a platter. Sure, my teammates had tied one on any chance they had, but I couldn't risk making a fool of myself, or worse, ending up passed out somewhere. But watching the businessman at the bar chug a beer, I suddenly wanted one—mainly to ease the piranhas in my stomach. While my brain was on overdrive about baseball, worry over Kade, and the possibility that I could be pregnant, I was freaking out about my grandfather's parole. What could I possibly say to keep my grandfather behind bars? I mean, the fact that he tried to have me killed should have been enough to keep him locked up without parole.

Shoes clicked along the shiny tiled floor, breaking my concentration. I glanced at the sharp-dressed man in a pinstriped suit with a pink shirt and bright-green tie.

He set his briefcase down next to Kade, who was sitting on my left. "Lacey Robinson?" He stuck out his manicured hand. "I'm District Attorney Brandt."

Kade popped to his feet, as did I.

After we shook, the three of us moved into the bar and sat at a table.

Mr. Brandt got down to business. "I don't have much time. I appreciate you meeting with me." He pulled out his phone and set it on the table. "I'm going to record this conversation if that's okay?" He set his blue eyes on me.

I swallowed hard. "Sure."

Kade slipped his hand in my lap.

Mr. Brandt tapped a button on his phone. "Tell me, Ms. Robinson, why you think Harrison Lorenzino should stay behind bars."

Rubbing my throat, I cleared it. "The man is a murderer. He killed my mom and sister."

"Technically, that's not true," Mr. Brandt said.

I straightened. "My grandfather hunted me down, had me kidnapped, and then threatened to kill me if my father didn't give him what he was after." I'd said the very same thing in a statement to the FBI right after they had taken my grandfather into custody. "More than that, he did have a hand in killing my mom and sister, even though he wasn't the one to drive the knife into both of them repeatedly." Darkness encroached on my peripheral vision. I squeezed my eyes shut for a second. "He deserves to live out his full sentence in prison."

Mr. Brandt's phone rang. He glanced at the screen. "I have to take this." He lifted the phone to his ear as he hurried into the lobby area.

"Breathe," Kade said.

I inhaled a large amount of air before slowly blowing it out. I had learned many years ago that breathing exercises helped to calm me until I met Kade. Then he was the one who soothed me.

Kade rubbed my leg. "I know this is hard, but you need to also tell Mr. Brandt about your PTSD and how your grandfather's release will have a great negative effect on you."

I wasn't so sure that my psychological state would be enough to persuade the parole board to keep the evil man behind bars. Still, I had to try.

Mr. Brandt returned, appearing distraught. His eyebrows were almost touching his hairline. "Well, this meeting is over. I just got word that your grandfather died this morning of a massive heart attack."

Holy crap on a cracker. I didn't know how I felt about that. I hated the man, but that didn't mean he should die.

Mr. Brandt collected his briefcase from the empty chair next to him. "I'm sorry for your loss."

I couldn't help but let out a nervous laugh.

Kade draped an arm around the back of my chair, not reacting in any way.

I looked up at the light above the table, thinking that my mom and sister had heard me when I'd said, "Tell those angels above to make sure my grandfather doesn't get parole."

I let out a loud audible sigh. Maybe things were looking up.

For the moment, I could breathe.

CHAPTER 7
KADE

I gnawed on my pinky finger as if it were my snack for the afternoon. My dad and I were waiting for Dr. Thompson, the neurologist who I'd seen in the past. When I'd gotten back from LA last Friday, I had immediately informed my old man that something was seriously wrong with me. I'd been experiencing a lot more dizziness and blurry vision as of late. I was also beginning to feel some weakness in my right arm. I had noticed it when I'd picked up the luggage at the airport. Considering I was having several types of symptoms, it was time to see a doctor.

My dad hadn't flinched or shown any signs of surprise when I'd told him about my symptoms. He had, however, not wasted any time in calling Dr. Thompson.

I would have been lying if I said I wasn't worried. I was terrified. But as I fidgeted in my seat, I kept thinking about Lacey and the possibility of her being pregnant. In one breath, I prayed she was. I wanted to start a family so damn bad, I could taste it. On the other hand, I didn't want to ruin her opportunity of playing baseball. We hadn't talked at all about pregnancy since that day at Dodger Stadium.

49

Instead, we had talked about her practicing with the Dodgers' Triple-A team. She'd made the decision shortly after she learned that her grandfather had died. Besides, she was still waiting for her monthly friend to appear.

My dad swatted my hand from my mouth. "Stop. You're about to drive me to rip off my own nails." If my dad was nervous, he certainly wasn't showing any signs as he sat there, poised and casually dressed in khakis and a crisp button-up shirt.

The waiting room was rather empty. Only one other person filled a chair adjacent to us—a woman in her late forties, I would guess. She was absorbed in a magazine. Maybe I should find something to read to take my mind off the exam, although Dr. Thompson wouldn't be able to tell me anything today, not without doing an MRI.

"Why didn't you come to me when your dizziness and headaches started?" Dad's panicked tone revealed for the first time that he was as nervous as I was.

"I just thought they were related to my usual migraines."

"What about the numbness above your eye?"

I pushed up a shoulder. "Comes and goes. But that is recent." I had started feeling the numbness at the airport as well.

"Does Lacey know you're here?"

I bounced my knee. "I'll tell her after I know what's going on." In my opinion, it was better to have all the facts. That way, she could concentrate on pitching without worrying about me.

My dad sighed. "Why haven't you proposed? I thought you were going to before her graduation?"

I chuckled. "I almost did. No, I didn't get cold feet. It just wasn't the right time."

"Son, there never is a right time."

I sat on my hands. "I want the proposal to be perfect and not overshadowed by anything like her grandfather's death or baseball. Besides, she doesn't want to get married for a couple of years."

He crossed one leg over the other. "So what? You can have a long engagement. Put that ring on her finger."

I wanted to. Actually, I wanted to whisk her away to Vegas and elope. Only her words had stopped me from proposing. *The major leagues might not want me if they know I'm married.* I knew that was a weak excuse. I knew all my excuses so far had been weak at best. If we loved each other, then she should say yes, no matter what was going on around us. Which led me to the only other conclusion—I had cold feet. I wanted an emphatic yes out of her when I asked. I didn't want any *buts* or *let's wait years* or *I can't be married while I'm playing baseball.*

"Kade Maxwell," an auburn-haired nurse said.

Dad tapped me on the leg as he rose.

I swallowed the nerves before I pushed to my feet.

"We'll get through this," Dad said. The panic that had resonated earlier was gone. In its place was pure confidence as though he knew I would be okay.

I wished I had his confidence. I wished I had his tenacity. I wished I had his strength. For so long, he'd been the anchor of the Maxwell family. He was the one who'd kept us from jumping off a cliff when my sister died. He'd been the one to hold his head high, hiding his emotions when my mom went to live in a mental health facility.

I could only nod, shoving down the tears that wanted to pour out of me as we ventured to the exam room behind the nurse.

Once inside, the nurse stabbed her pretty pink painted nail to the exam table. "Up you go."

Dad folded his tall stature into the lone chair.

The nurse grabbed a thermometer from the small counter by the sink before she stuck it in my mouth.

Dad snagged a magazine from the basket on the floor next to him.

I stared at the nurse's name tag that read, "Sheila."

When the timer on the thermometer beeped, Sheila said, "Normal." She then proceeded to take my blood pressure. Once she was finished, she jotted down the results on a piece of paper. "Dr. Thompson will be right in." Then she glided out like an angel.

Before the door shut, Dr. Thompson waltzed in. He wore a doctor's white coat over a blue shirt and striped red-and-blue tie. He stuck out his hand to Dad. "Nice to see you again, Martin." Then he set his brown eyes on me. "Kade, it's been a while."

High school had been the last time I'd seen Dr. Thompson after I blacked out from a migraine. Back then, he'd ordered an MRI, which had come back clean.

He planted his lanky body on a rolling stool. "So, your dad tells me that you're having numbness and weakness in the arms along with your migraines. Is the weakness in your right or left arm?"

I pressed the palms of my hands into the leather exam table. "Right. The numbness is on the right as well." I touched the area above my eye.

"Any speech problems, slurring, ringing in the ears, or hearing loss?" Dr. Thompson asked. "How frequent are the headaches?"

I stretched my neck. "None of the symptoms you just mentioned. In the last month, my headaches seem to be more and stronger."

He rubbed his smooth-shaven jaw. "Let's do a full blood workup and schedule you for another MRI as soon as possible."

"Do you think I have a tumor?" I knew he couldn't give me a straight answer, but I had to ask.

My dad cringed, the lines around his copper eyes deepening.

Removing his stethoscope from around his neck, the doctor began checking my heart and lungs. "I'm not going to speculate." He felt around my right arm before he instructed me to squeeze my hand into a fist. Then he whipped out a light pen and checked both of my eyes. "Any black spots in your peripheral vision?"

"Not at all," I said.

He tucked his hands into the pockets of his lab coat. "Does over-the-counter medication relieve your headaches?"

"I have to take four Advil, and even then, it only dulls the pain."

Dr. Thompson tipped his head at the door. "Let's go see Melissa out at the front desk. We'll get you scheduled for an MRI and CT Scan. In the meantime, I want you to take it easy. I also don't want you to drive. If for some reason you have an episode of dizziness or you start to see black spots in your vision, I don't want you behind the wheel."

My dad stood, shoving his hands in his pockets. "Lawrence, let's be frank. What are you thinking?"

I held my breath. I wasn't sure I wanted to know what Dr. Thompson was thinking even though I'd asked the question earlier.

"Martin, you know as a doctor that it's hard to give a diagnosis without test results."

My dad stared at Dr. Thompson as though he were trying to get into the man's head.

"Can I at least work?" I asked.

"As long as you're not operating heavy machinery," Dr. Thompson said.

Lifting liquor bottles or cases of beer wasn't heavy machinery. But I did need to find a ride to work.

As if my dad had read my mind, he said, "Between your mom and me, we'll get you to work. Plus, Kody is around too."

Dr. Thompson headed to the door. "Come on. I'll see you out."

The three of us walked down the hall to where a petite blonde typed away on her computer.

"Melissa," Dr. Thompson said. "Please set up an MRI and CT Scan for Kade Maxwell as soon as possible. Put a rush on it if you can."

She tapped some keys on her computer then picked up the receiver on her desk phone. Meanwhile, Dr. Thompson filled out a lab form for my blood tests. After he handed it to me, he said, "Fast tonight and get into the lab first thing in the morning."

"Can I have a word?" Dad asked Dr. Thompson.

"There's not much I can tell you, Martin, until the MRI results come back."

My dad angled his head at Dr. Thompson. "Humor me, please." Dad's tone was caustic.

Dr. Thompson narrowed his eyes at Dad as he flicked his head down a hall. The two strolled away, chatting.

I tuned them out as I waited for Melissa to give me the dates for the tests. My stomach pitched and rolled. What if I did have a tumor? I couldn't think the worst.

Melissa waved a small hand in front of me. "Mr. Maxwell?"

I blinked away the hell I was in.

"Friday morning is the soonest they had for both the MRI and CT Scan."

I shrugged, smiled warmly at her, and pushed down those tears that sat on the brim of my lower lids before I rushed out of the building as if it were on fire. Once outside in the hot sunshine, I almost collapsed from not enough air in my lungs.

Immediately, I pulled out my phone to call Lacey. With my shaky fingers positioned over the screen, my brain kicked into gear. I couldn't call her. I couldn't tell her that I could have a brain tumor or that something was seriously wrong with me. I couldn't put her on edge and ruin her day.

Idiot, just call her and tell her you love her. I refused to let her hear the fear in my voice. She would know something was up. Thankfully, my dad sauntered out, or more like marched out, with fear written all over his face. The last time I'd seen him with that look was when we moved Mom into a mental health facility.

Silence followed us as we wound our way to his car, dodging others who were going into the medical building.

When we were on the road, I finally broke the tension. "Did you get a straight answer out of Dr. Thompson?"

He slowed at a yield sign, his sight set straight ahead, his hands gripping the wheel as though he wanted to crush it.

I arched an eyebrow. "Did you hear me?"

He facial features were rigid. "I did." He pressed his foot on the gas.

A suffocating quietness filled the vehicle for the next several blocks.

Even though I wavered between wanting to know and not wanting to hear what Dr. Thompson thought, I still said, "Just tell me, Dad." My voice dropped. "I'm not a kid anymore. And this is my health."

Using the palm of his hand, he banged on the steering wheel, grunting in the process. "Son, you've never been a kid. You've always been the adult in the family."

"Then treat me like one," I snapped then slumped in the seat as regret washed over me. We were both scared. We were both thinking the worst. I shouldn't take out my frustrations on my father. At that moment, I was super glad I hadn't called Lacey.

Dad swallowed hard as he turned onto the country road. "He suspects that your scans won't come back clean. That was all he was willing to say."

I grabbed my throat with a shaky hand. It was as though I couldn't get air in my lungs. The word *fuck* was going off in my head like a damn tornado siren. I pushed the down button for the window and stuck out my head like a dog would, hoping the wind would jar me back to reality. Oh, wait. This was my reality.

Dad's large hand landed on my arm. "We'll get through this."

I pulled in my head. "You keep saying that. So how the fuck would we get through a brain tumor?"

Lots of gray had grown in on his sideburns. It was as if the gray hairs had just appeared when he walked out of the medical building. He set his watery gaze on me. "We need to hold it together and think positive."

I inhaled as a warm breeze trickled in through my open window. "I'm not sure I can. How in the hell am I supposed to tell Lacey? Or Mom? Or my brothers?" Each and every one of them would be devastated.

As the words left my mouth, the tears that I'd held so tightly from spilling seeped out. This couldn't be it for me. I was only twenty-two. I hadn't gotten married yet. I hadn't started a family. I hadn't even proposed to the one person who gave me a reason to breathe. Suddenly, I knew what I had to do.

"Dad, I need to fly to Oklahoma as soon as possible. I need to see Lacey. I'll leave after I give blood tomorrow, and I'll be back Thursday night." All the *what ifs* started to flood my mind. What if I didn't get the chance to propose? What if she was pregnant? Would I see our kid grow up?

Dad gripped the steering wheel, his knuckles turning as white as the car in front of us. "You can't go down there and scare her. We're not saying anything to your mom or brothers yet, either. We need to wait until we know more."

I couldn't promise him I wouldn't tell Lacey. Then something she'd said at the cemetery in LA made me sweat. *"Don't ever leave me."*

Fuck.

More tears flowed. "Promise me something, Dad. Promise me that if anything ever happens to me, that you would take care of Lacey."

He banged on the steering wheel again. "Fuck, Kade. Stop thinking like that." My dad hardly lost his shit unless it came to family. He swerved hard, pulling off to the side of the road along a ditch. After he shifted into park, he set his fury-filled eyes on me. "Listen to me." His tone was as hard as the large rock ahead of us. "Go see your girl. Propose to her. Make love to her. Laugh with her. Watch her live her dream. But under no circumstances should you bring her down. Do not tell her what Dr. Thompson suspects. We don't want to get her upset for nothing. Do you understand?"

I nodded like a scared boy, swallowing the grit that had somehow settled in my throat. I knew how to erase the emotions from my face. Hell, I was the king of the deadpan look. But with the possibility that my health might be compromised, I wasn't sure I could wear a happy face.

Dude, you've done it a million times after Karen died so your brothers wouldn't feed off your despair and depression. Somehow that was different. I'd been trying to help them move on from Karen's death; I had not been potentially facing my own demise.

I quietly recited a prayer, put a smile on my face, and squeezed my dad's hand. "I'm strong. I will be okay."

Boy, that was a big, fat lie.

CHAPTER 8
LACEY

The scent of fresh-cut grass always centered me. Yet for some reason, it did nothing to soothe the knot in my stomach. Since I'd arrived in Oklahoma the day before, I couldn't eat. If I did, I was running to the bathroom to dump the food I'd just eaten. I swore the opportunity to practice with the big boys and a potential contract looming were the reasons I couldn't keep food down.

Even as I strutted out onto the field, I wanted to heave. I'd never been more nervous in all my life. I scanned the stadium, my mind in a haze, matching the late-afternoon air. I squinted at the sun that sat just over the centerfield wall.

Breathe, girl. Just breathe.

I couldn't help but remember the first time I'd walked out onto the college ball field and how the fans had cheered and called my name. But the sounds around me were nothing more than the crack of a bat or the thud of a ball hitting the catcher's glove.

"Robinson," a deep voice called before the man's shadow crossed in front of me.

58

I blinked.

A gnarly hand waved. "Warm up." The scary voice belonged to Doyle, the pitching coach I'd briefly met earlier that morning.

I gave a slight nod before I jogged into the bullpen with Doyle on my heels.

A red-haired guy was tying his cleats, while the catcher flicked his chin at me.

"Hi. I'm Eric." He tipped his head at the red-haired guy. "That's Gil."

Gil raked his gaze over me, giving me a creepy feeling. I wanted to roll my eyes but refrained. The last thing I wanted to do was start trouble. Instead, I waved. "I'm Lacey."

"We know who you are," Gil said in a snippy tone.

Bite your tongue. You're being interviewed by the team as much as you are by Brice.

I couldn't say I knew many of the players. The only person on the team I'd met before was Santos, who was the captain and shortstop. He'd played for the Pawtucket Red Sox when I'd practiced with them two summers ago. I was confident I had at least one person in my court.

"We don't have all day, Robinson," Doyle said. "Let's see that arm of yours."

Eric squatted down behind the home plate in the bullpen. He flashed his blue eyes my way and threw me a ball. "Let's do this, Lacey."

Catching the ball, I gave him a once-over. His black hair and blue eyes reminded me so much of the triplets—Kelton, Kross, and Kody. Suddenly, those nerves that had taken over my body quieted as I twirled the ball in my glove.

Doyle went to stand down by Eric but off to the side. He crossed his short arms over his chest. "Start with your fastball."

Gil let out a snide chuckle. "She can't pitch."

Without looking at the jerk, Doyle said, "Cut the crap, Gil."

I'll show him what I can do. Asshole.

Eric donned his catcher's mask before I wound up and launched a fast pitch. The ball was high and wild and soared over Eric's head to hit the backstop with a loud thud.

"See," Gil said. "She doesn't belong here. She'll probably puke on her next pitch."

News traveled fast. But my stomach was telling me that Gil might have been right. As Eric picked up the ball, I glanced out. Men were in the outfield. Someone was pitching, and Santos was at bat. I inhaled as the tall Latino captain hit a home run.

You can do this. You know the game. Don't let men like Gil get to you. I certainly knew how to handle people like him. I'd had my fair share of bullying in high school with Aaron Seever, and I'd made it through his psychological games. Still, I was contemplating why I'd said yes to Brice's offer. Part of me felt Tony and Holly had outvoted him, and Brice was only going through the motions.

"Trying to figure out where to throw up?" Gil's snide tone grated on me.

Doyle grunted.

I whipped my head around and snarled. "I'm trying to decide if you're really an asshole or just plain scared that I will show you up. Oh, wait. You are an asshole. So I guess you're afraid of me."

He jumped to his feet as fast as a jackrabbit, his freckled face turning red to match his hair.

Eric jumped into action, blocking him. "Sit your butt down." Then Eric said to me, "Don't fuel his fire."

I raised my hands. "As long as he doesn't fuel mine."

"Enough," Doyle said in his deep and scary voice. "Now pitch, Robinson."

Eric got into position as I went through my pitches—sliders, curve-balls, and fastballs. Meanwhile, Gil had a permanent snarl on his face as he watched me throw ball after ball. I threw several wild pitches along with several great pitches, and I kept pitching until Doyle sauntered over to me.

"Now get out there," he said. "You're up. Eric, go and catch for her."

Eric and I jogged out. I wanted to say something to Gil, but it wasn't worth it. As I headed out to the mound, all eyes were on me. Suddenly, my hands began to shake, and I bit my lower lip that was so chapped it burned when my tongue touched it.

I slowed to a walk as Eric went ahead of me. The stadium seemed to be closing in as my cleats pounded into the soft, grassy right field. A sense of loneliness enveloped me. *What the hell?* I had no idea why all of a sudden I felt as though I didn't belong. Maybe I was tired of bullies and always trying to prove myself. After all, major league baseball had always been a man's game. *They aren't going to sign me.* At least that was what my intuition was telling me.

Eric backtracked. "Lacey, don't wig out now. You've got great pitches. You can do this."

I had to have a deer-in-the-headlights look. I stopped just as I was approaching the mound and swung my gaze to Brice, who was standing outside the dugout. One of his cheeks bulged out as he chewed then spit. I couldn't tell if he was concerned or not. I would bet he was waiting for me to puke or screw up. After all, he didn't believe the Dodgers were ready for a female. Or maybe what he'd been really trying to say was that *he* didn't want a girl on the team.

"Why are you not pushing me away or making snide comments like Gil?" I asked.

One side of Eric's mouth turned upward. "I believe that this game can be played by both men and women. Just because it's been a man's game for so long doesn't mean that a woman of your talent can't play with us. You're good, Lacey Robinson. Show them. Show Brice. And fuck Gil and whoever else is in his court."

I swallowed back the tears I desperately wanted to release.

Santos strutted over with his glove in hand. "Nice to see you again, Lacey. Are you ready?"

Eric slapped me on the back. "She is."

I wished I had his confidence.

Santos regarded me with his dark eyes. "Good, because the media is lining up."

"I think I'll be sick," I mumbled.

They both chuckled before Eric placed the ball in my glove. "Romero is batting. He hates fastballs. So throw him that ninety-mile-per-hour ball you've thrown to me."

"Focus on Eric," Santos said then moved over to the shortstop position.

"Remember, we're just practicing," Eric tossed over his shoulder while trotting to home plate.

Brice met me on the mound, his expression screaming *don't prove me wrong.* "Do we have a problem?"

I shook my head as the word no lodged in my throat.

"Good." His jaw began working as he returned to his spot near the dugout.

I froze on the mound like a damn statue. I was practicing. This wasn't a game. This was the moment of my life. This was the only chance I had to prove to these men that I could play the darn game. Yet somehow that feeling of loneliness was still front and center. Images of Kade and me in the bathroom at Dodger Stadium flashed before my eyes. Our conversation about me being pregnant was swimming around in my head. If I were pregnant, then the opportunity to play would be over. I would never get the chance again to try out or show a major league team my skills. They would worry that I could get pregnant again. I couldn't blame them. I also couldn't see myself pitching with a big belly and didn't know if a doctor would even let me play.

Stop thinking all those thoughts. You're here now. Pitch. As Eric said, you're good.

The long-lens cameras from the two photographers near the visitors' dugout were positioned steadily at me as though guns were drawn on me, and for a beat, a shiver danced up my arm. I guessed word had gotten out that the Dodgers were entertaining signing a woman to their roster.

In any case, I couldn't worry about the media. So I abandoned the cameras and eyed Eric. Then I dug my cleat into the dirt around the mound and fingered the ball in my glove. Sweat trickled down my neck as I settled in to throw a fastball.

Romero, who was waiting to bat, took a few practice swings before settling his stance.

The team around me tittered and shouted at Romero. I couldn't make out what they were saying. All I could do was inhale and exhale as my hand started shaking. I searched the empty seats, wanting nothing more than to hear the roar of the crowd. At least with a deafening sound, I wouldn't hear all the voices in my head that kept telling me I should be home, I shouldn't be here, I couldn't do this. Yet other voices were saying the opposite. Blackness crept in on the sides of my vision as though the sun had set. I shook my head several times. A panic attack threatened.

Santos's voice trickled into my ears. "You can do this."

I could.

I thought of home, Kade, my dad, my brother, Mom, and Julie. I got the feeling Mom and Julie were with me. At least they'd answered my prayer not to let my grandfather get out of jail. I hadn't expected him to die. I couldn't say I was sad, though, that he had. But I wasn't there to think of my grandfather and how I hated the man. I was there to do what I did best—pitch.

So I checked the field, a habit any pitcher had. After one sweep of the players who were staring at me intently, I readied my stance, gripped the ball, and finally threw a fastball.

The ball narrowly missed Romero's head, soaring past Eric, and hitting the backstop.

I dared not look around. I didn't have to when Gil's voice shouted something derogatory from the bullpen.

Asshole.

Eric returned the ball. I circled the mound once then twice. I would've thought Santos would've given me a pep talk, but he was quiet, as was everyone else. In fact, I could probably hear a pin drop.

I scolded myself as I gripped the ball. Then I eyed Romero, who was waiting as though he were bored.

Well, that pissed me off.

I nodded to Eric, who punched the inside of his catcher's mitt. Then I threw another fastball. This time, it went straight down to home plate.

Romero swung and missed.

I sighed heavily, and when I did, all the tension that had built up inside me escaped.

The guys on the field were still quiet, even Santos. I itched to turn around to see if Santos was still there. But I decided to keep my focus ahead of me.

Pitch the ball and show Brice that I am one of the best pitchers out there. I twirled the ball in my glove as I waited for Romero to step inside the batter's box. When he did, he squinted his light-colored eyes at me.

Cocking my leg high and tight, I threw Romero a wicked slider. The ball hit Eric's glove as Romero swung at air. He growled.

For the next ten minutes, I settled in and pitched as if I were taking my last breath. The finally tally—Romero hit two of my pitches in the outfield, hit four foul balls, and swung at air five times.

Then Brice called the team in.

Santos jogged up to me. "Nice pitching." He wrapped long fingers around my bicep. "How does a girl throw that hard and fast?"

I giggled, the act freeing. "You asked me that when you played for the Sox. And my answer then was the same as it is now—hard work."

As we trotted up to join the team that had surrounded Brice, I'd done my best for that day.

64

"Great practice," Brice said to the team. "We're ready for tomorrow's night game."

I wished I had the chance to play in that game. Or maybe I could if Brice signed me today.

Brice spit his nasty chewing tobacco. "Have a great night. I'll see everyone here tomorrow afternoon."

The guys dispersed, along with the coaches, leaving me alone with Brice.

"Well done, Lacey," he said.

"I know it's only one practice, but when will you make your decision?" I'd shown him what I had in LA and now. He also had tapes from my college games.

He took off his hat and scratched his matted head of dark hair.

"Why are you afraid to sign me?" I'd almost asked if he was afraid I was pregnant. But if I had, then I would have to answer him, and I couldn't give him a yes or a no. Besides, I didn't want to ruin my chances. I knew he couldn't ask me outright because of discrimination laws. Not only that, the reporters came over, sticking microphones in our faces.

A short lady with the ESPN logo on her mic smiled at me. "Lacey Robinson, how does it feel to play with the big boys?"

A young KTLV reporter in a suit shoved his mic toward Brice. "So are you going to sign a female?"

I held my breath. *This ought to be good.*

Brice's jaw worked hard to chew his tobacco, then he swallowed. "The details of our negotiations are not open to the public." He nodded at me then walked into the dugout and disappeared down into the tunnel.

I was left with the two reporters and their cameramen.

"What was going through your head when you were on the mound?" the reporter from ESPN asked as she flipped her brown hair over her shoulder.

I was about to answer her with my usual answer about deciding on the pitch, when I caught a glimpse of a tall, honey-color-haired man standing in the first row of the stands behind home plate.

It couldn't be my sexy hunk of a man. But as I reoriented my vision, I lost all train of thought.

The reporters followed my line of sight.

Kade waved with a thigh-squeezing grin on his face.

I pushed past the reporters and, on shaky legs, tried to sprint the short distance up to Kade. But he beat me to the punch as he strutted down toward me, dressed in tattered jeans that hung low on his hips. His hair was slightly damp, and he had a smile that warmed my heart so much, I wanted to cry tears of joy.

The closer he got to me, the more my heart raced and my body shook.

Five years with this man, and I still got the swarming butterfly feeling whenever he was near me. Even more so when he cupped my face, lowered his lips, and kissed me as if he were on his last breath.

Any feeling of loneliness vanished.

CHAPTER 9
KADE

I kissed her as though we'd been separated a lifetime. She returned the kiss with more feeling and vigor than I'd ever remembered from her. Or maybe it was all in my head. I couldn't think about anything but her on the plane ride down. I'd tried to erase the day before, dump any notion of a tumor into my brain's trash bin, but Dr. Thompson's words to my dad, "I suspect his scans won't come back clean," hadn't left my head until now.

I squeezed Lacey so fucking tight I thought I might break her. Then I inhaled her citrus scent that always made me feel as though I could conquer anything. "You were amazing out there." Whatever was about to happen to me, I knew without a doubt that I had to fight like a motherfucker to stay alive. Lacey would never survive if anything happened to me, and that thought alone would kill me before any brain tumor.

She leaned away, grasping my face in between her delicate hands. To this day, I wondered how her skin stayed so soft. "You saw me pitch?" Her voice hitched as love and excitement swam in her beautiful eyes. "I didn't see you in the stands, although I wasn't exactly aware of much except my pitching."

"I hung behind the reporters," I said. "Besides, I only caught the last half of your performance."

She let go of me. "What are you doing here? Not that I'm complaining."

I'd almost come with her, but she had insisted that this step in the so-called interview process was something she had to do on her own. If it weren't for my doctor's appointment, I might have argued otherwise, but she was doing much better now that her grandfather had died.

She eyed me as though she knew something was wrong. "This is a big step for you, and I wanted to be here in case you needed me."

She studied me. "My PTSD is fine. What's really going on? This is the second time you've surprised me."

She knew me too well. The first time I'd shown up at her dorm had been to propose. Now I didn't know whether to propose or tell her about my upcoming tests and what Dr. Thompson speculated. I didn't get a chance to do either.

The reporters rushed over, and the lady from ESPN stuck a mic in Lacey's face. "Lacey, you didn't answer my question. What was going through your head when you were on the mound?"

The dude holding the KTLV microphone watched Lacey intently.

She interlocked her fingers with mine. "When I'm on the mound, my mind is focused on pitching, nothing more."

"So do you think that the Dodgers will sign you?" the KTLV reporter asked.

She smiled, sucking in her bottom lip. "I'm not going to guess. I'm here to do my best. I'm sorry, but I'll be here tomorrow to answer more questions. Right now"—she glanced up at me—"I have a date." She tugged me.

I went willingly as we started for the dugout.

The ESPN reporter and her cameraman climbed the steps behind the visitor's dugout up to the first level of the stadium.

The KTLV reporter faced the camera and began talking. "Lacey Robinson, potentially the first female to enter a major league organization, has completed her first day of practice. The question now is will the Dodgers sign her and make history? Stay tuned. We'll be here tomorrow to bring you more of Lacey Robinson and her performance on the mound."

When we reached the dugout, Lacey asked, "Shall we go back to the hotel?"

That sounded fantastic. We could get naked and enjoy each other for the night. But as I glanced around the stadium and the cityscape in the distance, I had something else on my mind.

The KTLV men gathered their equipment and left the same way as the ESPN gal.

"Before we head to the hotel, let's take a walk." She'd always loved to stroll around after a game when we were in high school.

She studied me as she did earlier with questions written all over her face. "Okay." Her tone was hesitant as she took my arm.

The ballpark was big when sitting in the stands, but standing on the field, it felt small, cozy almost. I was beginning to understand why Lacey felt a sense of peace and excitement anytime she was on the field.

As we padded down the first baseline, I was trying to decide whether to break the news to her about my tests. My old man had counseled me not to tell her until we knew what the results showed. I wasn't sure not telling Lacey was good advice. I'd always gotten into trouble with her when I had kept things from her in the past. In fact, she'd broken up with me one time because I'd held too much back. I'd consistently kept her in the dark about things, and the last straw had been after I blacked out from a migraine and landed in the hospital during our senior year.

"I know you, Kade. Something is wrong. Are you worried about my PTSD? Is that why you're here?"

Stopping in centerfield, I touched the velvet box in my right front

69

pocket. "I don't want to be apart from you anymore. Four years was too long." Regardless of what I was keeping from her, I was totally serious. "Actually, it was hell." As much as I wanted to settle down and raise a family, I would go to the ends of the earth for her, even if that meant following her around the country as she played ball.

She let go of me. "I'm only here for a week."

I traced my finger over one of her sun-kissed cheeks. "Let's go to Vegas tonight and elope." Eloping had crossed my mind, but I hadn't expected that to come out of my mouth.

Her eyes were wide. Her jaw fell open.

"Before you answer, hear me out," I said. At least she wasn't protesting. That was a win. "I know you're hesitant to get married because the team or any team might get nervous that marriage means kids." The possibility of her being pregnant was still on the table, but I pushed on. I would get to that next. "They don't have to know we're married."

She walked in a circle, craning her neck up at the clear blue sky.

Her silence made me shiver and not in a warm and tingly way. So she wouldn't see my hands shaking, I dipped into the pocket of my jeans and latched on to the red velvet box, while my heart beat a staccato rhythm. "Say something, baby."

She closed the distance between us. "Something is going on." Frustration rode her tone. "Normally, I would give you space until you were ready to tell me." She shook her head. "I can't. Please talk to me."

I swallowed the big hairball that was stuck in my throat. Whether I had bad news to tell her or not, that fact didn't overshadow that I'd wanted to marry her ever since the day we graduated from high school. In the last month since her graduation, my mission had been to propose. At first, I hadn't wanted it to be on the baseball field. I wanted to separate the proposal from what she valued most. Yet as I looked at her beautiful face, I knew we were in the perfect place.

I sighed. "I've been waiting for four years for us to be together. I've been waiting that long to marry you. I don't want to wait any longer,

Lace." I placed a hand on my heart. "I want to carve another heart tattoo on my chest. I want to make it official that you are the reason my heart beats."

She removed her ball cap and gave me a sad smile, which felt like a blow to my chest. "I can't go to Vegas. I have practice tomorrow."

I shouldn't have been surprised at her answer even though it hurt like hell. "So did you get your period yet?" I vaguely remembered she had said her monthly friend was due this week.

A bevy of emotions crossed her face as she blew out a breath. "I'm due on Friday."

"Do you think you're pregnant?" Some women knew their bodies well or could tell when something was going on.

She shrugged. "I think it's premature to say yes or no."

Fair enough, although I was sure she had given me a vague answer because she didn't want to either get my hopes up or stomp on my wish to start a family. Not only that, we were similar in a lot of ways, particularly with giving each other bad news. She might have been holding out on the pregnancy thing, and I was not telling her that my migraines might be more than a headache.

Aside from the dull drone of city life outside the stadium, silence stretched between us. I swept my gaze around the park. A couple of men were emptying the trash can near the dugout.

When I oriented my vision back to Lacey, I found tears slipping down her face.

"Hey, baby. Now it's my turn to ask you what's wrong." I caught a lone tear with my finger.

Licking her lips, she lowered her gaze to her cleats then back up at me. "For the first time since Julie and Mom died, I feel empty and alone. When I walked onto the field earlier, I got this feeling that I'm not in the right place. I don't know if it's the vibe Brice is giving me. I should be beyond excited to be here." She waved her hands around. "I'm not, and I don't know what that means."

She was breaking my fucking heart. "You're not alone. You've got me."

She swallowed hard. "I know. But I'm scared of failing. Scared of losing you. Scared of our lives changing. I'm tired of trying to climb a ladder only for the rungs to be taken out when I reach the last step at the top."

I tipped her chin up to look at me. "How would you lose me?" Her words at the cemetery again pummeled into me like a fast-moving storm.

She lifted a shoulder. "I don't know. I just get this feeling that a rug is about to be yanked out from under me. I had the same cold feeling at the cemetery in LA."

She had to have a sixth sense. Regardless, a sharp pain spread through my chest. She was gutting me in more ways than one.

"I told you I'm not going anywhere," I said in the most confident tone I could muster.

She gave me a sad smile. "I'm afraid, Kade. I'm afraid I can't have it all—marriage, kids, a career in baseball."

Whether this was a good time or not, I pulled out the red velvet box.

She slapped a hand over her mouth.

"You *can* have it all. I'm not pressuring you. But whether you say yes or no, I've been dying to do this since I surprised you at your dorm the day before graduation." With slightly trembling legs, I got down on one knee. "Lacey Robinson, from the moment you pulled a gun on me in the high school parking lot, I've never been the same. You've unlocked my heart with those green eyes of yours. You make my stomach flutter anytime I lay eyes on you. You give me purpose that life is worth living. I'm hopelessly in love with you." I held the closed box in the palm of my hand as if I were serving up a delectable dessert. "We don't have to elope. We can have a long engagement. I'll wait for you forever. Marry me?"

Tears streamed down her face as she divided her attention between the box and me.

I, on the other hand, was ready to pass out because she wasn't saying anything.

Her fingers went around the box before she slowly brought it up to eye level. As soon as she opened it, she closed it.

"It doesn't bite," I teased.

Her hands began to shake as she opened it again. The waning daylight hit the ring at just the right angle for the diamonds to sparkle.

I'd picked out a setting that was simple yet elegant. Small diamonds fanned out along the band, and a one-carat center stone was nestled inside a circle of more diamonds that the jeweler had called a halo-style setting. Halo seemed perfect for my baseball beauty.

I rose, took the ring out of the box, and held it up, waiting for her answer.

She sniffled then smiled so fucking wide, tears shot out of my eyes. In that moment, she was the most beautiful creature that I'd ever laid eyes on.

She nodded her head rapidly. "Yes. Yes. Yes. I will marry you."

I slipped the ring on her finger. I knew it was the right size. I'd found a ring of hers in her bedroom at her father's house and took that with me to the jeweler.

She held up her hand, the diamonds shimmering. Then in a flash, she tackled me. "I love the crap out of you, Kade Maxwell."

I full-on laughed, releasing all the tension that had settled in every one of my muscles. "That's my line."

We both laughed, and no matter what happened from there on out, I would always cherish that moment.

CHAPTER 10
KADE

As I waited for Dr. Thompson to come in, I reminisced about the conversation Lacey and I had had on the ball field in Oklahoma. I was still trying to get my mind around why she'd felt lonely. Maybe I should've moved with her to Maine after high school. Maybe I should've attended more of her baseball games. Despite the marriage proposal and her saying yes, part of me was feeling as though I'd failed her.

She's over the moon, dude, at your proposal. I knew she was. That night after I'd proposed, she couldn't stop looking at the ring.

My knee moved up and down, much like it had the last time I was in Dr. Thompson's office. Only this time, I was bouncing both my knees.

My dad, who was in the chair next to me, placed a hand on my leg. "Stop."

I let out a nervous chuckle, or more like a snort. "How can you be so calm?"

I'd had my MRI and CT Scan earlier that morning, and my dad had pushed to have the tests read immediately. I had to thank him. Otherwise, I wouldn't have been able to function over the weekend, not knowing what the results were. Not only that, I wouldn't be able to keep any of this from Lacey. She was due home at any moment. Her old man was picking her up at the airport while I waited to hear good news or bad.

"Why can't you pick me up?" she'd asked.

"My dad wants my help with something," I'd said.

I was so in trouble with her for lying. *Schmuck. Asshole. Pathetic.* Those words described me well. I only wanted to protect her. I only wanted her to be happy. *As soon as you see her today, you have to come clean.*

A roar of laughter resonated in my head.

"Did you hear me, son?" Dad's voice broke through the war raging inside me.

I blinked.

"Whatever is about to happen, we'll get through it. You're strong. I'm strong."

"Lacey isn't," I said.

Dad turned in his chair to face me. "You know that's a lie."

I laughed. "You're right. But she's going to freak if my tests don't come back clean. I should've told her. I just couldn't, though." She'd been sad about feeling lonely. Then her demeanor had changed after I proposed. I couldn't have severed her happiness. "I did propose, and she said yes."

My dad grinned so big, my heart opened a little. "Congratulations. Now you two can plan the wedding. Your mom will be thrilled."

Oh God. Mom? I wanted to believe my mom was a strong woman. To a certain extent, she was. But the one thing she worried the most about was losing her sons. She'd lost her baby girl, and that alone was what had sent her into a mental health facility.

As though my dad knew what I was thinking, he said, "Your mom is strong too."

I swallowed an elephant as I stared at Dr. Thompson's diploma and other accolades and awards on the wall behind his desk. "I'm not sure *I* can be." If I showed weakness, then it would only send my mom and even my brothers into that depression they knew so well.

The door creaked open.

I took in a deep breath. My dad adjusted in his seat.

Wearing a smile, Dr. Thompson circled his large mahogany desk and nodded to Dad and me before he folded his stature into his chair.

Suddenly, the air in the room thickened, or maybe there wasn't any since I was having trouble catching my breath as my heart tried to break through a rib.

Dad leaned his elbows on both knees. "And the verdict is?"

Dr. Thompson smoothed a hand over his perfectly coiffed gray hair. Then he brought his hands to his mouth in prayer style.

I wondered for a split second if that meant I should start praying. Regardless, I did begin reciting those prayers that Mom had made us boys say just before bed when we were kids.

Dr. Thompson swung his gaze to Dad then me. "Kade, you have a medium-sized mass on the front right side." He touched the temple of his own head.

My jaw came unhinged. I felt as though he had just sucker punched me once, twice, three times.

Dad grabbed my arm. "When do you operate?"

Every muscle in me stiffened like a two-by-four.

Operate? Medium-sized mass? What the fuck?

Dr. Thompson held up a hand.

I wanted to take that hand and ram my fist into it. Granted, it wasn't his fault I had a mass.

I got up. "I need air." I needed more than air. I needed Lacey. I briefly closed my eyes, working hard to get my pulse to slow.

I am strong. I have to be strong. I have to fight this.

My dad caught my arm. "Not yet."

I dropped my jaw. "I can't breathe." I had to escape the four walls and the sunny atmosphere. A credenza banked one wall and was filled

76

with photos of Dr. Thompson and his family. My gaze landed on his little girl with blond pigtails.

A slew of several swear words shouted in my head as I thought that I might not ever get to have kids.

All of a sudden, I wished more than life itself that Lacey was pregnant.

"Kade," Dr. Thompson said. "Please sit."

I stood behind my chair, gripping, or more like crushing, the wooden frame as I replayed the conversation Lacey and I had had in the cemetery in LA.

"Don't ever leave me," she'd said.

"I'm not going anywhere," I'd said.

What a total fucking lie.

I shoved my hands through my hair, pulling on strands just to wake me the fuck up and get me out of my poor state of mind.

"The scans show you have a meningioma," Dr. Thompson said. "It's a type of tumor that is categorized as benign in ninety percent of the cases. However, they usually start out small. What's surprising is these types of tumors are not that common in young men of your age. Regardless, in some instances, a meningioma can be life threatening. Considering your symptoms, I'm concerned. We should remove the mass as soon as possible."

I suddenly hated that word—mass. I rubbed my hand on my chest where the five hearts were tattooed, as though it were my way of wishing all this away.

"The last two days, I hardly had any blurriness in my vision or dizziness or even weakness in my arm," I said in a cracked voice.

Dad got up and came around to stand next to me. "Son, the good news is we know what's going on. As Dr. Thompson said, ninety percent of the time, the tumor is benign. However, we shouldn't take chances and wait."

"Because of that ten percent that it might be cancerous. Right?" I had to throw that out there, but when the words left my mouth, I wanted to curl up in a corner and cry. The odds were stacked against me. Young men of my age were not likely to have a meningioma. But I did. Ninety percent of cases were benign, but I didn't feel as though I fell into that percentile, which made the bile rise to settle in my throat.

Dad rested a hand on my back. "Let's not think that way." Then he regarded Dr. Thompson. "How soon can we get him into surgery?"

"First availability would be next Wednesday," Dr. Thompson said. "Or we can schedule the surgery out two weeks, which is the next time available."

I shook my head. "I don't want to wait." I wanted to get on with my life. I wanted to get married. I didn't want to worry if the mass would grow or if my symptoms would get worse. I didn't want Lacey or anyone in my family to not be able to sleep for two weeks, either.

I blew out a long breath, wondering how I would tell Lacey. I checked my watch. Her plane had landed about an hour ago, and she should've texted me by now. I fished in my jeans pocket for my phone but came up empty. Then I remembered I'd left it in the car on the charger.

Dr. Thompson pushed to his feet. "I'll get everything set up. Melissa will be in touch with the details. For now, go home and relax."

My face twisted in every possible way. Relax? Easier said than done. I nodded at him anyway then said to my dad, "I'll wait for you in the car."

He tossed me the keys with a tentative smile. I was sure he had a ton of questions to ask Dr. Thompson, anyway. As for me, I didn't have any. I just wanted to get all this over with.

I ran out of the building as if I were running from a madman chasing me with a knife. I didn't stop until I got to my dad's car. My hand shook as I gripped the door handle. I stepped back and turned one way then another. I closed my hand into a fist, ready to punch something, anything. Doing so wouldn't take away the mass. I leaned against the car and slid down until I was sitting on the warm pavement. I stared at the shiny red car parked next to mine. I couldn't make out my reflection, but I would bet fear was painted all over my face.

I labored for air as the tears dropped onto my jeans one after the other.

Get your shit together, dude. Get your ass up and face the music. Get over to your fiancée's and tell her the news. Tell her you love the crap out of her and make love to her like it's your last day on earth.

More tears spilled.

A phone ringing drew me out of my funk. I looked in both directions before realizing that it was my phone in the car.

I climbed to my feet. The ringing stopped. I rubbed my eyes before I got in the passenger's seat. Then I picked up my phone.

Missed call and two text messages. I opened up the texts from Lacey.

Where are you? I'm home, and Becca is coming over. I've asked her to be my maid of honor. When you get this, call me.

The second message read, *Oh, and the Dodgers haven't made a decision yet. And I love you.*

I stared out the windshield at the back of a minivan, my brain working overtime, wondering how I was going to break the news to Lacey, or if I even could.

CHAPTER 11
LACEY

I dropped my bags on the hallway floor at my dad's house.

Dad fiddled with his keys as he padded into the kitchen. "I can't stay. I have to run by the Cave. I'll be home later, and we can have dinner."

I followed behind him and went down one step into our family room then plopped on the couch.

Dad came into the room. "I'm sure you're exhausted."

That was an understatement. I was in great shape. Physically, I could push myself past the soreness and pain. Yet my tiredness had more to do with the emotional strain since I'd learned of my grandfather's parole. Granted, I didn't have to worry about him anymore. Trying to impress Brice was the main reason I was emotionally drained at the moment.

I'd left Oklahoma with Brice's comments lingering, which didn't sit well. "We'll be in touch within a week or so."

My sixth sense told me his answer and that of the management team would be a big, fat no. *"We're not ready for a female"* was the answer I was preparing myself for.

80

Whether or not they would sign me, I'd done my best. I'd put every ounce of energy into my pitching. So much so that I swore I'd never worked harder.

For now, I wanted to table baseball. I'd been on warp speed since I'd moved to Ashford in my senior year of high school. Since then, baseball had been my major focus. Maybe that was the reason I'd been a little depressed and feeling sorry for myself. I hadn't given myself a chance to enjoy my family and Kade and my friends. I was chalking up that feeling of loneliness I'd had on the ball field in Oklahoma to my recent visit to Julie's and Mom's graves.

I gazed at my beautiful and sparkly diamond, kicking myself in the proverbial ass for telling Kade we should wait until my career took off before we even considered marriage. The minute his face brightened after I'd said yes was the minute I yelled at myself.

Even if I did have a career in baseball, we could still get married. If a team didn't like that, then that was their problem not mine. They had to treat me like every man on the field who got married. They also had to realize that I was an adult and managed my own career. So if I wanted to start a family, then I would, although I still believed that the Dodgers signing me was a long shot. All I could hear in my head was Brice saying they weren't ready for a female on the team.

I chewed on my lip.

"Something wrong?" Dad asked, drawing me away from my analysis of my career.

"I'm not sure I want to play for the Dodgers."

He reared back. "They're your favorite team."

I twirled the ring on my finger. "I don't want to play for a man who doesn't want me there. My manager has to be supportive, and I'm a little tired of fighting the war of men who don't think a girl can play baseball or a team that's not ready for a female player."

Creases dented his forehead. "Do you think other teams might be interested in you?"

I shrugged. "Not sure. But I wouldn't mind playing for the Red

Sox." It would keep me closer to home. That way Kade and I wouldn't be apart as much. He would also have his family nearby.

Suddenly, I thought my eyes might've bugged out.

"What is it?" Dad asked.

I straightened. "I'm going to call the Red Sox scout." John Gleason had been the one to invite me to spend time with the Pawtucket Red Sox two summers ago during my college break. I shouldn't wait for a team to come to me. I should go to them.

Dad smiled. "Great idea. I got to run." He started for the door.

"Dad, before you go, can I ask you something?"

He halted in his tracks.

"We haven't had a chance to talk about your father. Are you sad he's dead?" I couldn't say I was. But Harrison Lorenzino was blood and my dad's father.

Anger colored his cheeks. "I don't wish death upon anyone, but I'm not." As fast as the color surfaced, it vanished before his green eyes brightened. "It's time to shed the past. While you're waiting to hear from the Dodgers, why don't you plan a wedding? I know Kade is dying to marry you." He left through the kitchen.

A tingly feeling consumed me at the mention of the wedding. I had no idea how to plan a wedding. I had no idea where or when Kade and I would tie the knot. All I knew was I wanted to marry Kade as badly as he wanted to marry me.

Then as if someone threw ice on me, I realized today was the day I was supposed to get my period. Then again, I wasn't always on time. Some months, I was a day or two late; other months, a day or so early.

The doorbell rang followed by the creak of the front door. "Lacey, it's me, Becca."

"I'm in the family room."

Heels clicked on the hardwood floor before a gorgeous girl with bluish-black hair sashayed in, dressed in tight-fitting jeans with holes just above her knees. Her long white shirt hung to mid-thigh, and the words *Nurses Rock* were sprawled across her chest. Black ankle boots completed the outfit. Her face was made up as though she were about to hit the town or model for some big-time magazine.

"Whoa! Becca Young, is that you?" The last time I'd seen Becca was over New Years two years ago. Since then, we'd only spoken on the phone or exchanged emails every so often. We had both been so busy with college.

She set the handful of wedding magazines down on the coffee table as I jumped up to give my best friend from high school a huge hug.

"I've missed you," I said.

"Oh my God. You don't know how I've missed you."

As I eased back, I spotted the diamond stud in her nose. "Since when do you do piercings?"

She rolled her dark eyes. "Since Tyler dared me."

Tyler Langley had been in love with me in high school, and Becca had been crushing on him then. It had been a little tense when Becca found out that he was interested in me and not her. Still, I had no interest in Tyler other than friendship. My eyes had always been on Kade from the very first day I'd met the sexy hunk.

I sat back down in my warm spot. "Are you two still dating?"

Frowning, she got comfortable on the couch next to me. "Nah. We went our separate ways about two months ago. I know I should've called you and told you, but with college graduation, things have been crazy. So the good news is I got a nursing job at the local hospital here in Ashford."

I squealed. "Seriously? That's awesome. Kody's girlfriend is a surgical nurse there. Well, when she's not in the recording studio with my dad."

"Kody has a girlfriend? Whoa! I've missed a lot. First though, let's talk wedding. Then you can fill me in on all the Maxwell news and Lacey news." She leaned over and dragged the wedding magazines toward us.

I reached out and touched her leg. "I'm sorry about you and Tyler."

She waved me off. "It's all good. He was my high school crush, and

I had a chance to date him. Now I'm over him." Her tone seemed off, as though she were still hurting over the breakup.

I thought about prying, but if it were me, I wouldn't want anyone to open up an old wound. So I said, "I'm here if you want to talk about it."

She stuck out her chin. "Thank you, but I've spent years crushing on the boy who is now an ass in my book."

Somehow I couldn't wrap my brain around Tyler being an ass to her or anyone. I tossed Tyler aside and got us a couple of sodas before we settled in to catch up on the last couple of years of our lives.

For the next two hours, we talked endlessly about college, the Maxwells, her nursing studies, how she was excited to move back home, and how happy she was that she would be working at the local hospital. I listened and nodded and shared with her the highlights of my college career, which were all about baseball. Then I added in the Dodgers and my grandfather.

After a huge sigh, I hugged a small square pillow. "So I might be pregnant."

She had just brought her glass of soda up to her lips and froze. Her eyes widened.

"Might," I reiterated.

She set the glass down on the coffee table. "Are you late? Are your breasts tender? Do you have any nausea?"

I touched my breasts. "Not tender. But I've had some nausea." I proceeded to tell her about my embarrassing display on the mound at Dodger Stadium. "Oh, and I'm not late yet."

The front door opened then closed before Kade's voice filtered our way. "Lace?"

Becca and I glanced at the arched doorway leading to the hall until Kade's muscled body appeared.

Becca waved then whipped her head at me.

My body tensed. I'd never seen Kade so distraught before. He seemed as though he'd been crying. Kade never cried. My badass boyfriend had always had his shit together, even when I was blacking out or having a panic attack.

Kade swung his gaze from me to Becca. "I need to talk to Lacey alone." His voice shook.

Becca didn't waste any time. She got up, grabbed her purse off the coffee table, and hugged me. "Call me later." She ambled up to Kade. "It's great to see you." She tossed a worried look over her shoulder before she walked out.

When the front door clicked shut, my heart stopped. Kade hadn't moved. I tried to get my legs off the couch, but I didn't think blood was pumping through me.

Finally, Kade took in a deep breath and made his way over to me. He eased down into Becca's spot. "I need to tell you something." He puffed out his cheeks.

My stomach knotted. "Did something happen to your mom?" His mom had had angina, and maybe the ailment had progressed.

He scooted closer to me. His big body suddenly made me feel claustrophobic. His hand found mine. "It's not my mom. It's me. I have a brain tumor."

Blackness swept into the sides of my vision as I clutched my chest. "I'm not sure I heard you."

A tear ran down his face. "It's a meningioma. The doc says they're normally benign. My mass is at a good size where he's concerned. So he wants to operate."

My pulse pounded in my ears. The blackness started taking over my vision. I knew a panic attack was imminent, but I couldn't let it happen. Kade needed me. For so long, he'd been there for me when I blacked out or had nightmares. He was the one who had always worried about me. I did worry about him, but not as much. After all, he was the protector, my protector. He was the one who took care of me. He was the one who took care of his brothers and his family.

Oh my God. I'd been such an idiot. He had traveled to Oklahoma because he'd known he had a tumor. That was the reason he'd appeared as though something bad had happened. I should have been angry he hadn't told me then, but the shock in my body was overpowering all my emotions. Besides, arguing wouldn't change the fact that he had a tumor.

"That's why you came to visit me. Isn't it?"

"Come here." He grabbed my hand and nudged me to sit on his lap.

So I straddled him then slumped my shoulders before I allowed the tears to flow.

He kissed my hand. "I didn't know. But the doc suspected that my scans wouldn't come back clean."

All of this was making sense. He was pale when he'd shown up at my college dorm. He staggered that day when he'd gotten out of bed. He'd been rubbing his temples more frequently. I attributed all that to his migraines.

"So it wasn't just headaches you were having?"

"The dizziness was getting more intense, and I've had other symptoms like weakness in my right arm."

So I wouldn't pass out from the onset of a panic attack, I leaned in and kissed him. At first, my lips brushed over his until he became a crazy man as if he were never going to get the chance to kiss me again.

I pulled away and started bawling. "You can't leave me."

He tugged me to him, rubbing my back. "I'm not going anywhere, baby. I can't. We have a life to build. We have a family to start. We have to grow old together."

He only made me cry harder.

"Make love to me," he whispered.

I couldn't deny his request. I didn't want to, either. He was the love of my life, and I needed him more than ever. Yet as we shed our clothes, I couldn't help but think that this could be our last time together.

When we were naked and he was on top of me, he said, " No matter what happens, I want you to play baseball." He nibbled lightly

86

on my chin. "I know I've been a little pushy on starting a family, but we only get one chance at life, and we should live it."

I snaked my hands around his waist. "You're right. But we do things together. Baseball isn't the end-all."

"I want you to live your dream, Lacey Robinson."

"You are my dream, Kade Maxwell, and I will not leave your side."

He entered me slowly and steadily, and as soon as he was all the way in and our bodies were moving in sync, I let the tears flow as I memorized every part of him.

CHAPTER 12
KADE

I made love to the one woman I wanted forever with. She moaned and cried and moaned and cried, but each time she whimpered, my chest tightened.

I stopped moving and gently dragged my hand down her warm, wet cheek, staring into her eyes. So much sadness lived in her cloudy green irises that I almost started bawling. I locked my jaw tight. I'd done enough crying before I'd gotten there. I had to be strong. I had to think positive thoughts. Besides, the stats were in my favor, or at least I had to believe they were.

She flattened her palms on my jaw. "We'll get through this." Her voice wasn't that convincing.

I got up and dressed. As much as I wanted our intimate prelude to continue, I couldn't bear to see the despair written all over her pretty face no matter how much I wanted to feel every part of her. And some part of me said that this wasn't the last time I would make love to her. This wasn't it for me.

I buckled my belt as she sat naked with her hair messy, looking like a fucking angel. Nope, I couldn't leave this earth or her. I wouldn't.

88

She rose and snaked her arms around my waist. "I will be strong for you, for us."

A noise in the kitchen made me flinch. Then I realized her old man could be home. I checked behind me.

She sniffled. "My dad isn't home." Then she began to dress.

I lowered myself to the edge of the couch, threw my head in my hands, and sighed.

She pressed a hand to my back. "Let's go to Vegas and elope."

I jolted up. "Seriously?"

She blinked away tears as she gleaned the wedding magazines. "It's too overwhelming to plan a wedding. We can get married now, and when things settle, we can have a party."

"But what about baseball?"

She buttoned her jeans. "Baseball has consumed me. It's time to let loose and build that family you want."

I raked my gaze over her, my eyes landing on her stomach as a bolt of hope zapped me. "Isn't today the day you're supposed to get your period?"

She gathered her long hair and twisted it up on her head. "Let's not worry about that. I just want to get married."

I couldn't help but wonder if she wanted to rush to get married because of my news. I would like to say it didn't matter. After all, I'd wanted to jet off to Las Vegas only a few days ago. But I got the feeling I was somehow forcing her hand to tie the knot sooner than she wanted.

"Did the Dodgers not sign you?" When I'd left her in Oklahoma, they still hadn't given her an answer.

She sat on the coffee table in front of me. Then she slid her hands up my thighs. "Whether they do or not, my life is about us, not baseball."

Her words were music to my ears, but I couldn't help but remember the conversation we'd had right before I'd proposed.

I grasped her hands as though she were my lifeline. Hell, she was.

But I needed her to be happy. I needed her to want marriage as much as she wanted baseball, and even though her words said her life was not about baseball, I wasn't sure I fully believed her.

I brought one of her hands up to my lips. "Baby, you can have kids, marriage, baseball, all of it. I don't want you to have to settle on one thing. Any baseball organization who respects your talent will work with you when you get pregnant."

One side of her mouth turned upward. "I know."

"We probably shouldn't run off to Vegas, either. My mom would be devastated if she didn't see us get married." She'd been so excited when I told her that morning that I'd proposed to Lacey.

She gave me a slight nod as my phone buzzed. I fished it from my jeans pocket and opened the screen to find a text from my dad. *Son, I need you to come home. I've called a family meeting. Bring Lacey.*

I showed her the text. She hopped up and found her shoes.

"You'll have to drive," I said. "My dad dropped me off."

Within minutes we were out the door.

All the way to my parents' house, we held hands as she kept her other one on the steering wheel.

When we finally parked in the driveway and got out into the late-afternoon sunshine, she said, "I had a weird feeling in the cemetery in LA. Now I know why."

I draped my arm around her as we walked into the house. "I believe you have a sixth sense."

"Maybe I'm psychic," she cooed with a little happiness in her voice.

I chuckled for the first time in days. The feeling felt as if someone had taken a suction hose and sucked out all the bad mojo inside me. Maybe that was a sign that I fell in that ninety percentile. Still, things could go wrong during the operation, and with that realization, I tensed as we entered the house and then the dining room. I became even more anxious when I laid eyes on Kelton, Kross, Kody, and Mom.

Oh, fuck!

I had to break the news to my mother. If anyone wouldn't survive the news of my tumor, it would be my mom. I regarded my dad, who had his chin up and shook his head once at me as though he knew what I was thinking. From my mom's calm expression, I knew my dad hadn't told her a thing.

I wondered for a minute where Kross's wife, Ruby, my niece Raven, and Kelton's girl, Lizzie, were. But I quickly shucked that thought. I was certain Kross and Kelton had rushed over from Boston as soon as my father had called. Kody lived in town, so his trek was minimal, and I would bet his girl, Jessie, was working.

Kelton scanned me then Lacey. "You two look like shit."

No one else said a word. Anytime my dad called a family meeting, we knew it was something big.

My mom's blue eyes widened as fear overpowered that calmness she'd had a moment ago.

Lacey squeezed my hand. "It's going to be fine."

"Wait," Kody said, his attention on Lacey's left hand. "Bro, you've finally proposed?"

A loud squeak came out of my mom, and all that fear vanished in an instant. "Martin, is that why you called the boys to come home?"

The fright on my dad's face said otherwise, but no one noticed as Mom and my brothers crowded Lacey and me with kisses, hugs, and congratulations.

"You know, Dad," Kelton said, "the news of Lacey and Kade's engagement wasn't enough to get Kross and me to speed down the highway and drop everything we were doing."

"Yeah, Dad," Kross chimed in. "What's really going on?"

I didn't blame my brothers for questioning my dad. I would've too.

My mom, who had her arm around Lacey, lost her smile.

Fuck me.

"Everyone," I said, "let's sit."

My mom went back to her chair next to my dad. "Martin." Her light voice took on a high-pitched sound.

Lacey tugged me to a chair at the head of the table, opposite my dad. My brothers filled the three chairs on my right. Lacey found the empty one on my left next to me.

Once everyone was settled, I opened my mouth, but nothing came out.

Lacey intertwined her fingers with mine in my lap.

I pushed out all the air in my lungs. "Well, there is no easy way to say this."

Dad held up his hand. "Kade, wait. I'm the patriarch of this family. I'll start." Dad considered my mom. "I called this family meeting because what I have to say can't be said on the phone." He then acknowledged my brothers. "First, I want to say I'm sorry that Kade and I haven't said anything up until now. But we had to be certain before we could share the news."

"Honey," Mom said in a frail voice. "Just come out and say it."

It was my turn to hold up my hand. Dad had taken on too much of the burden in times like these. Not to mention, he seemed to be struggling, which was not his MO. As strong as he was, he always seemed to hide his feelings to ensure that our family saw his confidence.

"Over the last month or so, I've been having some symptoms that I thought were just part of migraines." I watched my mom, who was riveted on me. "This morning I had an MRI and CT Scan on the advice of Dr. Thompson. It turns out that I have what they call a meningioma, which is a mass here." I touched the right side of my head, above my temple. "Ninety percent of the time, they're benign." I didn't want to scare my mom any further, seeing the fright on her face.

Nevertheless, a sharp intake of air came from my mom.

"Fuck," came out of Kelton's mouth.

"Martin," Mom said. "Is this true?" She knew my dad didn't call a meeting for nothing. She also knew my dad wouldn't subject her to news like this unless it was true.

Dad reached out to grasp my mom's hand. "I'm sorry, honey. Kade does have a mass. It's probably nothing to worry about. This type of tumor grows on the surface of the brain rather than within the brain. Hence, why they're mostly benign."

Tears welled up in Mom's eyes. "It's that ten percent that scares me."

I went over and sat in the empty chair next to her. "Mom, I'll be fine. I have a great doctor, and nothing is going to happen to me." Even though something could happen during surgery, I still had to instill the belief that I would be okay, maybe more for myself than anybody else.

Jumping on my bandwagon, Kody chimed in. "He will. I feel it in my gut."

I jerked my head toward Kody. He was the brother who had brooded and mourned for years over the death of our sister then his high school sweetheart. He'd been the one to run and hide at bad news. He was the brother who would immediately jump to the worst-case scenario. He was the brother who always believed that bad luck followed us. As of late though, he'd been a changed man, thanks in part to his steady girl, Jessie.

Kody rolled his shoulders forward. "What? I do."

Lacey giggled. Her laugh was contagious as everyone but Mom laughed and agreed with Kody.

"He's right," Lacey said, her voice soothing my frayed nerves. "Kade isn't going anywhere. He has to marry me first, and we have to make lots of babies."

Again, laughter filled the room, except Mom still wasn't convinced with tears in her dark-blue eyes.

My dad got up and kissed Mom on her head. "Honey, we're not losing another child. Kade is strong, and with the power of family, we'll get through this." My dad delivered those lines as if he were leading an army into battle.

"You promise?" Mom asked. "Because I wouldn't survive another death in the family."

All of us knew that very thing, and somehow a calm feeling washed over me. It wasn't my time. My mass was a hiccup in the road, and deep down, I felt that it would bring us closer together as a family.

Dad gently pulled Mom to her feet then wrapped his arms around her. "I promise."

As a doctor, my dad would never promise. As a husband, he would do anything to safeguard my mom's emotional state. I couldn't blame him. I was my father's son. I would do that in a heartbeat if it meant that Lacey would relax, although I knew my dad's words wouldn't ease my mom's worry.

She backed out of Dad's arms and gave all of us a tentative smile.

Then I hugged her. "You will not lose a son."

I had to believe my own words.

CHAPTER 13
LACEY

Kade was sitting up in a hospital bed with a smile on his face. The man was getting ready to have his brain worked on, and he was grinning. I, on the other hand, had a mild case of nausea. I'd been so freaking nervous the last five days. I couldn't sleep. I couldn't eat. And I couldn't even think straight.

I frowned. "Why are you so chipper?" His mood was a stark contrast to the night before when he'd tossed and turned along with me. Or maybe he hadn't slept because I'd woken up in a pool of sweat from a nightmare I couldn't remember.

With the passing of my grandfather, I shouldn't have been having nightmares. *Your fiancé has a brain tumor. It's natural to freak out.* Regardless, Kade had been taking care of me since he met me in high school. It was my turn to show him I could be strong for him.

I feigned a smile as I stood by the side of his bed.

You're failing miserably.

Kade grabbed my hand that was picking at the blanket covering him. "I know you're nervous. You know what's helping me take my mind off the operation? I keep thinking about our wedding and maybe that I might be a dad." He prodded me by raising his eyebrows.

Standing on the other side of Kade's bed, Mrs. Maxwell jerked her head at me, parting her red lips. At eight in the morning, the woman looked as if she'd just stepped out of a clothing shoot. Her black hair was twisted into a perfect bun on the top of her head. Light makeup colored her porcelain skin, and she wore a crisp cotton button-up shirt over a pair of black slacks.

I'd barely gotten dressed that morning. I was wearing jeans that hadn't been washed in a week. I'd grabbed the first pair I got my hands on in my closet, and I had on one of Kade's T-shirts. If I couldn't be with him, I wanted to at least feel as though I were. Plus, his shirt smelled like him, which was keeping me somewhat calm.

Mrs. Maxwell checked on her husband, who was standing near the door, typing on his phone, oblivious to our conversation. Then again, Kade's voice hadn't been that loud.

Still, I was five days late, and while I was experiencing a mild case of nausea, I didn't believe it had anything to do with a pregnancy. I highly suspected I was late because of the anxiety from everything going on—the stress of baseball, my grandfather, and now Kade's operation. I was ninety-nine percent sure I wasn't carrying his child.

Mrs. Maxwell brought her dainty hands to her lips in prayer formation. I would bet she was praying that I was carrying their third grandchild. Kross's wife Ruby was due with their second child in a couple of months. They'd announced the good news at Christmas.

She flashed her big blues at me. "Lacey, are you?" Her tone bordered on excitement of huge proportions.

I sucked in my lips, shaking my head. "I'm on the pill. So I don't think so."

"She's late," Kade said as though he were a hundred percent sure.

Kade's mom relaxed her features, or more like lost that radiant gleam in her eyes. "How late?"

I nibbled on the skin inside my mouth like a chipmunk eating a nut. "Only a few days. Please don't get your hopes up." I directed my statement more to Mrs. Maxwell. She'd been dying for Kade and me to get married and pregnant. The woman wanted lots of grandbabies. *Talk about pressure.*

She patted Kade's hand. "A few days doesn't mean anything. Women can be late for any number of reasons."

I released a quiet sigh. To be honest, I was all over the map on whether or not I wanted to be with child. Aside from baseball, Kade and I had to think about our finances. I didn't have a job. Kade did, and while my dad did pay him well, I didn't think his salary was enough to support us and a child.

"I'll take a home pregnancy test while you're under the knife," I said. It wasn't a bad idea to know either way. But again, I was almost certain I wasn't.

Kade opened his mouth to speak, when Dr. Thompson strolled in garbed in scrubs with a plaid cap covering his head. I hadn't met the doctor, but his name embroidered on his top gave him away.

Mr. Maxwell pocketed his phone as he joined Dr. Thompson at the bottom of the bed.

"Are you ready, Kade?" Dr. Thompson asked.

Kade mashed his lips into a thin line as he nodded. "More than ever."

"Good. A couple of things. You'll be given a local anesthetic. So you'll be awake during the surgery. Barring any complications, the operation should take a few hours. I can't say for sure an exact time." He regarded Mr. Maxwell. "Halfway or three-quarters of the way through, I'll have someone come out and give you an update. Any questions?"

I ran my tongue over the area of my bottom lip that I'd been chewing on. "What can go wrong?" *Please say nothing.*

Dr. Thompson flicked his gaze to me. "With any surgery, there is a risk of infection and bleeding. As I told Kade, surgery could produce some damage in the normal tissue of the brain, which can cause problems with your ability to think, see, or speak."

Kade and his dad didn't react. They had already been informed. Yet, Mrs. Maxwell and I exchanged a look of horror. I couldn't imagine not hearing Kade's raspy voice or listening to him tell me what he was going to do to me just before we made love.

"Dr. Thompson is an expert with this type of operation," Mr. Maxwell said to his wife in a calm and soothing tone.

I had no doubt that he was probably thinking how a complication could shatter her mental health much like Karen's death had.

A squat male orderly came in dressed in scrubs, a cap, and wearing a cheery smile.

"I'll see you in the operating room." Dr. Thompson tapped on the rail of the bed before he left.

Mrs. Maxwell kissed her son on the cheek. "The whole family will be here when you come out."

"Son," Mr. Maxwell said. "You got this."

Kade grinned at his dad. "I know."

I wished I had an ounce of their confidence.

The orderly readied Kade's bed for transport as I watched his parents leave.

"Baby," Kade said in his husky voice. "I'll be fine."

I snarled more at myself than anyone. I wanted that surety. I wanted to believe he wouldn't suffer from any complications. But after hearing Dr. Thompson, I was more apprehensive than when I'd walked into the hospital. "Argh! Why is everyone so sure of themselves?"

"Baby, it's out of our hands. It's now up to Dr. Thompson."

The orderly, whose name tag read Bob Garmin, said, "Dr. Thompson is a god when it comes to brain surgeries."

He better be, or else I will go crazy on the nice doctor.

Kade kissed the back of my hand. "See. Nothing to worry about."

I wanted to protest that if the tables were turned, he would be freaking out too. Instead, I leaned over and kissed him. Before I knew what was happening, we were tongue dancing.

Bob cleared his throat. "We got to go."

Reluctantly, I eased back. "I love you."

Bob wheeled the bed out, and my heart paused until Kade said, "I love the crap out of you, Lace. See you soon."

When he was out of sight, I began saying my prayers that I would hear his voice again, and as I did, I felt as if someone had sucked out my soul. I couldn't move. A part of me believed that he would be okay, but hell. He was about to have his brain tinkered with.

My hands trembled. So I clasped them together in front of me.

Stop thinking the worst. Instead go get that pregnancy test. Call the scout with the Pawtucket Red Sox that you had planned on reaching out to. Do anything to take your mind off of Kade's surgery.

I did need to keep my mind occupied somehow, or else I would end up in a hospital bed myself.

Mr. Maxwell's voice penetrated through my cloudy brain. "Lacey, let's get some coffee."

"You mean a stiff drink." I didn't drink alcohol, but I wanted to at that moment.

Laugh lines carved out the area around his mouth. "I could use one of those." He draped an arm around me. "Mrs. Maxwell is waiting for us."

At that moment, the emptiness I'd felt several minutes earlier vanished. I had a family—a future father-in-law who was like a second dad to me. A future mother-in-law who I considered my mom now. Plus, I had Kelton, Kross, Kody, and their significant others. My dad lived in town, and he wasn't going anywhere. Not to mention, I'd reunited with my best friend, Becca, and I had other friends I'd made during my college days.

We passed nurses and doctors as we met Mrs. Maxwell near the elevators. She stood like a queen amid the hurried medical personnel around her.

"So, have the Dodgers called yet?" Mr. Maxwell asked.

"Not yet. But I've been thinking of talking to the Red Sox."

He lowered his arm to his side. "That's great. You would be close to home."

Exactly my thought.

Mr. Maxwell stabbed the down button for the elevator.

When the elevator dinged, we piled in and took it down to the first floor. Once we got out along with several other hospital personnel, I said to my future in-laws, "I need to make a couple of phone calls."

Mrs. Maxwell touched my arm. "Are you going to buy that pregnancy test?"

Mr. Maxwell's eyebrows shot up.

She gave her husband a warm smile. "I'll tell you about it in a minute, dear."

For the first time in a long time, I let out a giggle. The tables were turned. Now Mrs. Maxwell and I were the ones confident and relaxed, while shock raced across Mr. Maxwell's aging face.

"I will," I said.

She entwined her arm in her husband's. "Good." Then they started in the direction of the cafeteria. "Lacey might be carrying our next grandchild."

"I have a feeling that the boys will be spitting out babies left and right," Mr. Maxwell said as his voice faded.

That was probably a true statement. Kross and Ruby were already on number two.

I wound my way out of the hospital and into the morning sunshine. I inhaled the scent of summer as I strolled down a sidewalk along the front of the hospital.

I tapped on Becca's name in my contact list. The phone rang four times before the line went to voice mail. "Hey, Becca. Can you pick up a pregnancy test for me and meet me at the hospital. I would do it, but I don't want to leave." She was headed to the hospital today anyway to pick up her schedule for her new job.

After I hung up, I sifted through my contacts for the number to the Pawtucket Red Sox's scout, John Gleason.

Red lights flashed as an ambulance pulled up to the emergency room.

I tapped on his name then watched the EMTs scurry to get their patient into the hospital.

The line rang twice before it connected.

"This is John," he said in a deep voice.

I cleared my throat. "Hi, John. I don't know if you remember me, but this is Lacey Robinson."

He chuckled. "Of course I remember you. The team still talks about you."

A good sign for sure. The team had been extremely welcoming and open to a female when I'd spent almost a month with them.

"So, I was wondering if the Red Sox would be interested in me. Maybe one of the minor-league teams." I didn't expect to walk on to their major league team. Most players started their careers in the minors.

I held my breath.

The line was deathly quiet.

I checked my screen to see if the call had dropped. "John, are you still there?"

"I'm sorry, I had to mute the phone when my assistant came in. So I hear you've been practicing with the Dodgers' Triple-A team. Are they interested in signing you?"

Sitting down on a cement bench, I watched the ambulance drive away. "News travels fast. Anyway, I'm waiting to hear back from them. I spent a week practicing with their Triple-A team." Brice had said he would be in contact within the week, and it had been a week. So I didn't think the Dodgers were interested. Frankly, I'd hardly thought much about them or baseball since Kade told me about his tumor.

The sound of John tapping keys reverberated in the background. "We're well over halfway through the season. The Sox's roster is full. But I can test the waters maybe for next season. That is if you don't get signed by the Dodgers."

My next call would be to Tony Greer now that I was thinking a little clearer. I would have called Brice, but I didn't have his number. The only time he'd called me was from the Dodgers' head office in LA.

"Thank you," I said. "I honestly don't think that I'll be signing with the Dodgers."

"Why not?"

"If they were really interested in me, they would've signed me when I was in Oklahoma." At least I believed that since they were in desperate need of a closing pitcher, and a team wouldn't drag their feet with games left in the season. "I understand that rosters are full. I would really appreciate it if you could test the waters as you say."

"Can I give you some advice, Lacey?" John asked.

If he said that I needed to rethink a career in baseball because I was a female, I might reach through the phone and punch him. "Sure."

I could hear him typing, or so it seemed. "I want you to talk to Tara Bannister. She's a sports agent and one of the best in the industry. She knows how to broker deals, and I believe you will like her. More importantly, if you want to make a play for the majors, you'll need an agent. I'll send you her information in an email, and I'll let her know you will be contacting her. Does that sound good?"

That was great advice. The Dodgers had asked if I had an agent. But I hadn't had time after graduation to do much other than talk to them. But I did need someone who had my back and best interests at heart, and if Tara Bannister believed in me, then I might have a shot at playing in the major leagues. "That sounds great."

"I'm glad to hear," John said. "I do think you will have a shot with a good agent."

My stomach fluttered for the first time in a while, and it wasn't a love flutter but a maybe-luck-was-on-my-side flutter. "Thank you."

"Look for that email," he said. "Good talking with you, Lacey. I have a meeting I have to get to."

I thanked him once more before we hung up. I was about to hit redial to the Dodgers' head office, when I realized it was around five thirty in the morning in LA.

For the moment, I went in search of the hospital chapel.

An hour after praying for Kade, I was feeling a little better—at least about my career and the possibility of an agent. I was in a one-stall bathroom, peeing on a stick, while Becca read the box that the test had come in.

"I'm not sure I can pee with you in here," I said.

She rolled her eyes. "I'm not leaving. I have the same female parts as you."

It wasn't that I was modest. Sometimes it was hard to relieve myself with someone watching me.

Becca turned on the faucet. "This should help you."

My mom had always done the same when she wanted me to pee before getting into the car for a long road trip. As soon as the water started flowing, the sound triggered my bladder. When I was finished, I set the test on the sink then washed my hands.

Becca threw the box into the trash. "With this test, you should get a yes or a no readout. So now we wait." She dipped into her big purse and produced a wedding magazine. "Want to look at wedding dresses?"

I raked my gaze over her. Her black hair was up in a ponytail. Her face was clear of makeup, and she didn't look as though she had aged one bit since high school. More than anything, she knew how to take my mind off of things. "I've missed you."

She stuck out her bottom lip. "Same here. Now that I'm home, we can hang out like we did in high school."

God, I would love that. I had three close girlfriends in college, but

Jennifer lived in North Carolina, Heather lived in Minnesota, and Peggy hailed from New Orleans.

"How many people do you want in your wedding party?" she asked.

I closed the lid on the toilet seat then sat down. "I haven't thought that far. But I would say three plus you." I wanted to ask Jennifer, Peggy, and Heather to be bridesmaids.

Becca darted her gaze to the test. Then it was my turn as my pulse sped up. I pushed to my feet as my palms began to sweat. The sound of us breathing filled the small space. When I blinked, the word became clearer as did the beating of my heart.

"Well, crap," Becca said.

I couldn't take my eyes off the test. As much as Kade and I weren't ready for a baby, part of me had warmed to the idea that I could be carrying his child. But as I suspected, the word on the test read *no*.

Becca hugged me. "It will happen one day."

I was elated yet sad. Kade and I were just beginning our lives together. We had so much to do before we brought a child into the world. On the other hand, having a baby would've certainly made Kade a happier man, and I definitely wanted kids. I couldn't wait to see if our kids had honey-colored hair like Kade or black like his mom. I mean, his niece, Raven, was the spitting image of his mom and her dad, with big blue eyes and the blackest hair.

Becca snapped her fingers. "Earth to Lacey."

I zeroed in on her pink nails. "I'm good." I was. I would be even better when Kade came out of surgery, alert and talking.

"Glad to hear because for a minute, I thought I would have to call a doctor in."

I rolled my eyes then looked in the mirror. My brown hair was frizzy. Dark circles marred the areas below my eyes, and I did look pale.

Becca wet her hands before she smoothed them over my hair. "Give me that band on your wrist."

I handed her the blue band. In a matter of seconds, my hair was in a bun on the top of my head.

Then she pinched my cheeks. "There. Now let's go see the Maxwell family."

I checked the time on my phone. Dr. Thompson had said he would send someone out to give us an update. I hoped I hadn't missed that. Then again, it had only been about an hour and a half since Kade had gone into surgery.

As we headed up to the second floor, I texted Mr. Maxwell to find out which waiting room he and Mrs. Maxwell were in. The last time I'd left them, they had been on their way to the cafeteria.

Before Becca and I reached the elevator, Mr. Maxwell sent his location. Within two minutes, Becca and I entered the waiting room where the triplets were sitting around, appearing sullen and tired.

Surprisingly, Kade's parents looked better than their sons. Maybe the coffee had kicked in for them.

Mrs. Maxwell came over to me. "Are you pregnant, Lacey?"

Becca snorted.

That one sentence erased any despair off the triplets' faces as their eyes widened.

I shook my head.

Mrs. Maxwell furrowed her eyebrows. "I'm sorry."

I hugged her. "Kade and I have a lot to do before we can have a baby."

Before any of the Maxwells had a chance to speak, Becca started talking a mile a minute. I giggled. I had missed her jabbering.

She fired questions at the triplets, asking when Kelton was getting married and saying how she wanted to meet Kody's girlfriend, Jessie. She kept them occupied as they filled her in on their lives until Jessie waltzed in.

Anyone who was sitting jumped up as the room fell silent.

Dressed in blue scrubs and a blue cap, she gave Kody the most loving smile before she spoke. "Normally, the crowd screams for me," she teased.

Becca's face scrunched.

"Jessie is a singer," I said.

Then the light bulb came on for Becca. I'd mentioned Jessie and her recording contract with my dad to Becca when she'd been at my house the other day.

Jessie scanned the room until her brown gaze landed on me. Some emotion washed over her, and I couldn't tell if it was sadness or fear. "Kade is doing well. It'll be another hour before he's out of surgery."

I clutched my chest as I closed my eyes for a beat, silently rejoicing that he was okay. But the tone of her voice said there was a "but" coming.

"Thank God," Mrs. Maxwell cried.

Becca latched on to my arm.

Kody sidled up to Jessie. "You're leaving something out."

All eyes centered on Jessie.

"Sweetie," Jessie said to Kody, "I'm not in a position to say more than that." Her tone slowly lowered as though she wanted to yell at Kody.

Kody crossed his muscled arms over his chest. "Baby doll, I get your job and the confidentiality, but if Kade is fine, then whatever you're holding back shouldn't be bad news."

"Son," Mr. Maxwell said. "Let's wait for Dr. Thompson. Kade is doing well. So there's no need to worry."

"Please, Jessie," I chimed in. All I could think about was that Kade wouldn't be able to speak anymore or see me.

Her chest rose before it deflated. "As I said, Kade is doing fine. But..."

And there it was.

"Please tell me the tumor isn't cancerous." I barely got that line out of my mouth.

Jessie tucked her hands into the pockets of her scrubs. "It doesn't appear so, but we'll have the tumor tested just to be sure. Kade lost consciousness, and we had to sedate him. Again, he's fine. We just don't know if there's any damage to the brain tissue. Dr. Thompson will explain in more detail when he's finished."

I collapsed onto a chair, feeling as if I'd gotten the wind knocked out of me. Damage to Kade's brain? If I made it through the next hour or however long the operation took, then I would classify that as a miracle.

CHAPTER 14
KADE

My eyelids were heavy as I oriented my vision. Bright lights above me made me squint. Beeps and voices sounded muffled around me.

"Welcome back," a familiar voice said. "Can you tell me your name?"

I knew the voice, but I couldn't place the name. I studied the nurse with brown eyes and a small nose.

I started an internal search, not only of who the nurse was, but where I was and what had happened. All I could remember was talking or counting, then I'd lost the ability to breathe before my body shook.

A man came up on the other side of my bed with a plaid cap on his head. I squinted at the doctor, trying to get my brain to fire on all cylinders. Another man drew up alongside the doc, and immediately his face registered.

"Dad?"

He grinned as his eyes filled with tears. "Son."

As if someone had injected my memory bank, I slowly began to remember. I scanned the nurse's face again. "Jessie?" I said her name more to myself.

As though the sound of her name out of my mouth was soothing, she let out a breathy sigh.

Then I eyed the man in the plaid cap. "Dr. Thompson?" Again, his name was more for me than for him.

"You gave us a bit of a scare. What's your name?" Dr. Thompson asked.

My dad watched, and I swore he wasn't breathing.

"Kade Maxwell."

All three of them blinked in slow motion.

Dr. Thompson's head bobbed. "Good. Now count to ten for us."

So I did. Afterward, I added, "My head is sore."

Dr. Thompson checked the monitor above my bed. "That's normal. You'll experience some mild headaches and feel tired. I'll prescribe some pain meds."

"What happened? One minute I was talking, and then next..."

Dr. Thompson gripped the side of my bed. "You had a seizure right when we removed your tumor. Seizures are quite common during brain surgery. So we put you to sleep and then stitched you up."

Dad wore a relieved and happy expression. "They were able to remove all of the tumor."

I should have been rejoicing, but I was too tired and groggy. Still, it was great news. Now I wanted to see Lacey. My gaze darted past my dad. All I could see was part of a bed across from me.

"Lacey," I said.

Jessie patted my arm. "You'll see her soon enough. We could only let one person in recovery, and that person had to be a family member." She gave me a sad smile.

Lacey was family, but I understood that technically she wasn't at the moment.

"She's fine, son," Dad said.

I shuddered a breath more out of relief than from remembering how frightened Lacey had been when the orderly had wheeled me out of the room. Luckily, my dad had been right outside, and I'd asked him to take care of Lacey. That was the only reason I hadn't jumped out of that bed to console her.

Dr. Thompson removed his cap. "You should rest." He glanced at Jessie. "Get him down to his private room. He can have visitors but not for long." He focused his attention back on me. "I'll check on you later." He gripped my dad's shoulder for a brief second before he left.

"How's Mom?" I asked.

Dad slid into Dr. Thompson's spot. "Everyone is well and dying to see you. I think your brothers were more worried than the rest of us."

Jessie readied me for transport. As she did, I closed my eyes. I was dying to see my family, but I was tired. I wasn't sure I could keep my eyes open.

"Rest for now," Jessie said. "It will be about thirty minutes before we get you situated."

The bed began moving. Dad was on one side and Jessie on the other. As they talked, their voices dulled while I fell in and out of sleep. Cold air washed over me as they wheeled the bed past nurses and other medical personnel then into an elevator before Jessie and Dad were pushing the bed into a cozy and somewhat dimly lit room.

"I'll need to hook Kade up to the monitor. You can get Lacey and Mrs. M.," Jessie said to my dad.

My eyes fluttered open as Jessie was fiddling with wires and pushing buttons on the monitor off to my right. Then she tucked me in. "Do you need more blankets?" She pressed a button somewhere until I was halfway up into a sitting position.

"I'm good for now." I had what felt like two heavy blankets on me.

Jessie gently grasped my arm then hung the wired control device over my bedrail. "If you need anything, press this button." She pointed to one of the controls. "I'll be back later to check on you."

She faded from my view as I drifted off. I didn't know how long I was out before a melodic voice called my name. Then cold but soft hands were on my face.

I opened my eyes, and the most beautiful woman came into view. I wanted to reach out and hug her, actually devour her, but I was afraid if I moved, my head would burst.

She must've sensed my struggle because she gripped my hand. As soon as my skin touched hers, an electrical charge zipped up my arm. I swore she had just infused me with her essence. The monitor that had been singing slowed.

She beamed from ear to ear as her meadow-green eyes sucked me in. "Hi."

Man, that sugary voice gave me another jolt of healing.

I hated to tear away my gaze from my fiancée, but my mom came up to the other side of my bed. Talk about a happy face. She was the epitome of joy. I didn't think I'd ever seen my mom with such a wonderful and bright smile.

My mom rubbed my jaw. "How are you feeling?"

My head felt sore, and I wanted to sleep, but I was still ready to jump out of bed and throw myself at Lacey and my mom. I was so fucking thankful and grateful that I'd made it through the surgery. In that moment, as my mom, my dad, and Lacey crowded around my bed, I let the tears flow as I grinned at each of them.

"I take it that those are joyous tears," Mom said through her own.

All I could do was nod.

Lacey giggled as she swiped a hand over one eye then the other.

Mom glanced at my dad. "We're going to run home and freshen up. Jessie will bring in the triplets in a bit."

Exhausted and haggard would have been words I would have used to describe my dad, even though he was smiling.

"Take your time," I said. "I'm not going anywhere."

Lacey squeezed my hand for dear life. "Neither am I."

Damn right she wasn't. Or else I would have to hunt her down dressed in nothing but a hospital gown and a bandaged head. I was sure no one would want to see me chasing her with my ass showing.

Once my mom and dad were gone, Lacey lowered the rail of my bed and climbed up on the edge, folding her leg underneath her while the other one dangled off the bed. "I'm going to be your nurse." She waggled her eyebrows. "I think when you get home, bubble baths are in order."

Hot and quick, a warm feeling shot down to my groin. "As long as my nurse is in the bath with me." Bubble baths with Lacey were epic. She would get in first, while I leaned over the tub and lathered her up, teasing and playing until she was at the point when she was about to climax. Then she would stop me from playing until I got in. Then she had her way with me, soaping me all over. I stopped right there. If I kept thinking of those times in the bathtub, I would be tenting my sheet for sure.

Settling her gaze on my groin, she arched an eyebrow. "We should talk about something else."

Fuck that. I wanted to close my eyes and replay bath time.

"I want to hug you and kiss you," she said. "But Dr. Thompson said you need your rest."

"He didn't operate on my lips," I teased.

She checked on my groin, smiling. "Let's wait on the kiss. A nurse might come in."

Considering I was getting hornier by the minute for some reason, I had to take it down a notch. Still, a kiss wouldn't kill me. I was about to protest, when she lost her smile.

"What's wrong?"

She lowered her gaze to her denim-clad knee. "I'm not pregnant. I think I was late because of all my stress over my grandfather, baseball, and then you." She sounded disappointed.

"You're sad about that? I thought you didn't want to get pregnant now." A dull pain sat heavy in my chest. I'd been hoping she was carrying our child.

She shrugged and sighed. "I warmed up to the idea. But we have so much to do before we have babies, Kade. I guess I'm feeling a little sad too because I know how much you want children."

"Baby, as much as the thought of you pregnant excited me, you're right. We do have a lot ahead of us. And I want you to live your baseball dream."

She frowned. "The Dodgers haven't called. The season is coming to a close and fast. But I did speak with John Gleason the scout for the Red Sox. I figured I would see if he could put in a good word for me with the Sox. He said he'd check on things more for next year, and he gave me the name of a good sports agent." Her frown vanished as her phone buzzed.

She removed it from the back pocket of her jeans. "It's the Dodgers office in LA." She gulped in air then answered. "Hello."

I couldn't hear the caller, but her frown was back.

"I understand. I appreciated the opportunity to work out with the team. Thanks again for your interest in me." She set the phone down on the bed.

Without thinking, I moved to wrap my arms around her and forgot about the IV. Not only that, the slightest movement made me extremely dizzy. Instead, I played with her fingers.

"That was Tony Greer. Brice and the management team have decided to go with another closer for the remainder of the season. As much as I knew their answer would be no, I'm still hurt."

Her pain became my pain. In my mind were the words *I want to hug you, but any movement kind of hurts.* What came out, though, was all garbled. I licked my lips and tried again. "Gu ou."

Her eyes went wide. "Oh my God. You can't speak clearly." She flew off the bed. "I'll get Jessie."

Her backside faded as my eyes closed. I repeated the sentence in my head. *I want to hug you.* Then I tried to say those words out loud. Again, gibberish.

"Kade." Dr. Thompson's voice resonated.

I opened my eyes and found Dr. Thompson standing over me. Next to him was Lacey, holding her finger hostage in her mouth.

"I want you to say the alphabet," Dr. Thompson said.

"A, B, C," I started. I finished with Z, not missing a letter.

"What were you trying to say to Lacey?" Dr. Thompson asked as he waved a light pen in my eyes.

"I"—I took a breath as I repeated the sentence again in my head —"I want to hug you." My delivery was slowed and slurred. But at least I could say the sentence.

Lacey cried. Behind her, I spotted my brothers waltzing in.

"Kelton, Kross, and Kody," I said more to myself.

Lacey whipped around and threw herself at Kelton, who was the first one to come in.

Kelton's arms went around Lacey. "Hey. What's wrong?"

Kody and Kross rushed over to my bedside, opposite Dr. Thompson, who was now looking under the bandage on my head. "Any headaches at the moment?"

"No," I said. "Dizzy, though."

He secured my bandage. "You need to rest. Everyone has five minutes to visit. Then I'm ordering you out." He pinned his gaze on Lacey.

"I'm okay?" I asked.

Dr. Thompson pocketed his light pen. "You are. Not uncommon to have some speech impairment right after surgery. But if you're experiencing severe headaches, I want you to push this button." He stabbed his finger at the wired control device Jessie had draped over my rail earlier. "Five minutes." He waved his hand at my visitors.

Lacey rushed over when Dr. Thompson left. "Tell me you love me. I want to hear it."

I had to say the words in my head first. Then I said it out loud. "I love the crap out of you."

She threw her head in her hands and cried.

My heart broke into a million pieces. Again, I recited my words silently before spewing them out. "I'm okay, Lace. You heard the doc. Normal stuff." I wished I could console her and pepper kisses all over her, but that would have to wait.

Thankfully, Kelton came up to stand beside Lacey, then he tugged her to him. "Shh. It will take an army to fuck up Kade, not some brain operation." His tone was light.

I nodded at my brother. Dr. Thompson was right. I needed to rest. Maybe with some sleep, my brain could recuperate.

Lacey shuddered a breath. "I was so afraid I would never hear your voice again or you say my name."

Silently, I repeated her name then gave it a shot out loud. "Lace."

When she beamed and her eyes lit up, I let out a huge sigh of relief. Everything was right in the world.

CHAPTER 15
LACEY

The Maxwell family chatted around the enormous dining room table. Four months had passed since Kade's operation. He was fully recovered. The speech problem he'd had right after the operation didn't happen again. I'd been worried just about every day afterward if his speech or his eyesight would fail or if his brain would swell. But according to Dr. Thompson, those complications usually showed themselves right after surgery. Since Kade's operation had been in July and we were now celebrating Thanksgiving, he was out of the woods, although he had an MRI scheduled after the holidays just to be sure there weren't any signs of regrowth.

While a recurrence of a tumor did sit in the back of my mind, Kade wasn't or hadn't had any symptoms, and his headaches had all but vanished. So we concentrated on spending time together with bubble baths, movies, family, and talking about our wedding plans.

Mr. Maxwell sat at the head of the table, clinking his glass lightly with his fork. Everyone was ready to dive into the three plates of carved turkey. Thanksgiving was always a fun time around the

Maxwells. The night before, we had gathered around a campfire down at the lake and said what we'd been thankful for during the year.

I was grateful for Kade's speedy recovery and grateful that his tumor had been tested with no signs of cancer.

The newest grandbaby, Reaghan, cried, stopping Mr. Maxwell from speaking and halting all conversation. Ruby popped to her feet and crossed the room to the bassinet. Reaghan was two months old and had the lungs of a great cheerleader.

Mr. Maxwell rolled his eyes. "Good to know that Reaghan can stop you guys cold and I can't."

Laughter bounced around the room.

"Papa," Raven said. "My sister needs food."

Again, laughter erupted. Six-year-old Raven Maxwell would be a force to be reckoned with as she got older. She was outspoken and had a wit about her.

Kade reached over and grabbed my hand. "I can't wait until we have kids."

Back in July, I'd wagered war with myself over my pregnancy scare. Being pregnant should be an event to celebrate when two people loved each other as much as Kade and I did. Yet I'd been scared and selfish. I was still a little frightened at becoming pregnant, but not because of baseball. More because I didn't know what to expect physically or if we could handle the financial side of having a baby.

Kade and I had agreed that before we had our first baby, I would give baseball one last push. So I'd contacted Tara Bannister, the agent John Gleason had recommended. We'd chatted several times by phone but planned on a face-to-face meeting after the holidays. She was very excited to represent me, and I was equally excited that I had someone who would do all the so-called dirty work in negotiations. That meeting with the Dodgers in LA had been more than nerve-racking, and I didn't care to go through something like that again.

For now, I was loving the time with Kade. Four years away from him had been way too long.

"Lace," Kade said in my ear. "Are you with us?"

I leaned into him, wanting to hear more of his raspy voice that I'd feared I would never hear again. "I'm here."

Reaghan had stopped crying, but Ruby was nowhere to be found. I suspected she was breastfeeding her daughter, who looked exactly like Raven, with black hair and blue eyes.

Mr. Maxwell glanced at his wife, who was sitting on his right. "Kids, your mom and I have an announcement."

As everyone around the table exchanged looks from surprise to interested, they settled in to hear the big announcement. I suspected they wanted to tell us about their upcoming trip to Belize, which Mrs. Maxwell had been talking about.

Across from Kade and me, Kelton draped his arm on the back of Lizzie's chair. The couple was still going strong. He hadn't proposed yet, but we all suspected he would when he finished law school.

Next to Lizzie, Kody regarded Jessie. The two had been hot and heavy for over a year now, and it was great to see Kody happy and in love.

To my right and close to Mr. Maxwell, Kross was adjusting Raven's booster seat. She still wasn't tall enough to sit in an adult chair to reach the table and eat comfortably.

"We should wait for Ruby," Mrs. Maxwell said.

"No, Mom," Kross piped in. "Go ahead. She might be a while. Reaghan eats like a horse."

"Very well," Mr. Maxwell started. "Your mom and I have purchased every piece of land within a five-mile radius of the house and around the lake."

Everyone looked at each other with puzzled expressions.

Mrs. Maxwell clasped her hands in front of her on the table. "Essentially, we would like to build each of you a house around the lake. It's our wedding gift to each of you."

I whipped my head up at Kade. "Did you know?" He and I had been discussing where to live. Since he was managing the Cave in town and I didn't have a job yet, my dad had offered his house. He was hardly there. So for now, it made sense to live at home.

"Dad," Kross said. "I can't accept that. That's way too much."

Kelton and Kody agreed in unison.

Kade's parents looked at him. He was the big brother, and usually the triplets followed when Kade made a decision. "He's right, Dad, Mom. Take your money and travel. Go do things you haven't done because you were raising us. Enjoy life. You've earned that."

Mr. Maxwell rubbed his clean-shaven jaw. "We knew all of you would protest. We've raised you to work hard, take nothing for granted, and put family first. And for that, your mom and I couldn't be more proud. We also know you have lives outside of Ashford. I'm not saying build a house tomorrow and move in. This proposition is a long-term plan as you grow your family. Think of the house and property as your summer retreats."

The gift was way too much. Mr. Maxwell had money, but money didn't matter when it came to family.

"Why don't we pay you a monthly rental fee or mortgage payment?" I asked.

Mr. Maxwell chuckled.

Mrs. Maxwell shook her head. "We insist on doing this."

Kody leaned over the table slightly so he could see his mother. "But Mom, four houses is way too much money. As Kade said, go enjoy yourself. You've been talking about Belize."

Her blue eyes flashed with intrigue as she considered his statement. "Your dad and I have already booked our trip to Belize for after Christmas."

Mr. Maxwell pinned a loving gaze on each of his sons. "If it makes you more comfortable to pay us, then we'll accept that. But your mom and I will decide on a monthly number. Fair enough?"

Kade and the triplets glanced at each other, while Lizzie and I raised our eyebrows. Jessie appeared indifferent. Between her nursing job and the recording contract with my dad, she was in a good financial situation. Kross had his boxing, which garnered him a good salary. As far as Kelton and Lizzie, they were both in college, trying to work and study.

The brothers nodded at one another. Then Kade spoke. "We agree."

Their parents radiated with happiness.

Then everyone dove into the meal, piling food onto their plates.

Our lives were coming together. So I shouldn't worry about how we were going to pay rent or a mortgage, at least not at that moment. So I unfolded my napkin, set it on my lap, and started in with our wedding plans. It was a perfect time to share with the family more details of where and when Kade and I would get married.

But as I opened my mouth to tell them the date, Lizzie spoke up. "Lacey, please tell us you and Kade set a date."

Everyone busied themselves with passing food or taking sips from their drinks.

Kade kissed me on the head. "We have. The date is set for the first Saturday in June."

"We want to get married down by the lake," I added. The area was big enough for a hundred guests or so.

Mrs. Maxwell buttered her bread. "Well, we were hoping you wanted a big wedding. We would like to invite some of our relatives on both sides of the family."

Kross whispered under his breath, "Keep it small."

I didn't want small. I was only getting married one time, and I wanted all my family and friends and the Maxwells' family and friends to celebrate our union.

"It's going to be a huge wedding," I said with so much giddiness in my voice, I could probably fill up the dining room.

Jessie and Lizzie squealed.

Ruby returned. "I heard a big wedding."

Mrs. Maxwell smiled, and my heart opened up.

Raven clapped. "Can I be the flower girl?"

"Of course. We were going to ask you." I grabbed my glass of water.

"Yay," Raven cooed.

Kade made as though he was kissing my ear. "You just made my mom the happiest mom on the planet. Thank you."

She was my mom too, or about to be. I loved her and every Maxwell hard, and I would do anything for them.

On that note, we talked, laughed, and ate.

It was time to marry the man who'd rocked my world that first day I met him in the high school parking lot.

CHAPTER 16
LACEY

People scurried around the backyard of the Maxwells, setting up tables and chairs. The five large tents and the wooden platforms had been installed yesterday.

Soft music pumped out of the speakers on the makeshift stage that Kody, Jessie, and their band-mate, Jake, would occupy during the reception.

I couldn't believe that my big wedding day was here. A floral scent floated in the air. The florist was setting vases of red and white roses on each table.

I swung my gaze from one side of the yard to the other. The florist's assistant was clipping the heads off colorful carnations down by the lake and tossing them on the water. Kade and I wanted the lake to be our backdrop, so I'd decided that flowers floating on the surface would be a pretty scene for our special day.

Past the floating flowers, the water glistened beneath the morning sun. A slight chill hung in the air, which was unusual for June, but I welcomed it. I'd been running around like a madwoman with all the planning and preparations.

Becca's voice trickled down from the garage. "Yeah, Mom. I will." She came up alongside me, pocketing her phone. "The transformation is amazing. I mean, this place has always been beautiful, but right now it's breathtaking."

I nudged her with my shoulder. "It's everything I dreamed about." Night after night, I'd lain in bed, thinking about my dress, the bridesmaid dresses, songs, flowers, vows, the weather, the food, and everything else that went into planning a wedding. Thankfully, Becca, Mrs. Maxwell, and Lizzie helped tremendously. I couldn't ask Ruby since she was dealing with a nine-month-old and Raven, and Jessie was handling the DJ duties.

Speaking of Raven, I couldn't wait to see her in her red-and-white dress. The color scheme I'd chosen was red for the bridesmaid dresses except Becca's. Her dress would be black. The men were wearing black tuxedos. Raven's dress was designed with a sleeveless white bodice, a red skirt that fell to her knees, and a satin black band that separated the top from the skirt. With her black hair, the color ensemble was perfect.

"I love the boathouse," Becca said, drawing me back to the present.

The wooden structure looked like a small house with a deck on one side. Red roses intertwined with baby's breath were woven into the deck's rail.

"I feel like we stepped into another world," I muttered, more to myself.

"So, have you seen the inside of the boathouse?" Becca asked.

I gave her a sidelong glance. Her chin was jutted forward, and she had a smirk that said I was going to love it. "I thought it was off-limits." Kelton had warned that if I even climbed one step, he would throw me in the lake.

I didn't think he would, or for that matter, I didn't think Kade would let him. But he had been dead serious when he'd delivered that message to me.

Becca lifted a T-shirt-clad shoulder. "So? I would've peeked." She giggled.

"Have you seen inside?" I asked.

She shook her head, her black ponytail swinging behind her. "Kelton would cut off my legs. He can be scary when he's determined to do something."

"I would hate to go up against him in court," I added.

Glasses clinked as workers held them upside down by the long stems, walking around to place the wine goblets on the tables.

I checked my phone. I'd been waiting all morning for Kade to reply to a text I'd sent as soon as I'd woken up that morning. "Kade and the boys should be back at my house by now." A tinge of concern edged my tone.

Becca positioned herself in front of me then grabbed the sides of my arms. "It's time to wake up Jen, Heather, and Peggy if they're not up already."

The girls had commandeered the Maxwell house, while the men in the wedding party had gone to Boston for a couple of days. They'd been due back in Ashford the night before. My dad had invited them to crash at his house.

I lifted my phone. "Let me call Kade one more time."

Becca huffed. "Kade is fine. He's probably hung over from all the partying he and Hunt and the rest of the groomsmen did last night."

Not Kade. He wasn't a party animal. His idea of fun was spending a quiet night with a few beers and hanging out with his brothers and his best friend, Hunt.

Becca knitted her dark eyebrows. "You're not still worried about a relapse of his tumor, are you?"

I angled my head. "Considering his latest MRI came back clean, no. But I can worry about my man."

My phone chirped.

Becca narrowed her eyes. "If that's Kade, you have two minutes to chat. We have hair and makeup, and we need to get those bridesmaids out of bed."

I showed her my screen as my phone kept ringing. "It's my agent. Hi, Tara." Tara Bannister was one of a handful of female sports agents in the industry. She'd been talking to several baseball teams on my behalf, although she hadn't had much luck in securing a meeting with any of them until last week. She'd said she might have something brewing.

"Are you ready for your big day?" Tara's voice was deep for a woman.

"As I'll ever be." My exasperated tone wasn't that convincing. "So you're still coming to the wedding?"

She let out a hearty laugh. "I wouldn't miss it. I'm calling to ask if I can bring a friend since I only checked one guest on the invitation."

"Sure," I said. "So, any news from the Red Sox?" With the season already in full swing, I wasn't holding out hope that a team would sign me. But two weeks ago, the Sox had lost their relief pitcher for the season to an injury, and they'd called up another pitcher from one of their farm teams, which meant the Sox could have an open pitching position.

Despite hoping, I had to be realistic about my chances. The Dodgers had opened my eyes to how difficult it was going to be for me as a female to play in the major leagues. Tara was convinced that the day would come when the big leagues would sign a female, but probably not as fast as we both wanted to see me pitch in a major league game.

"I'm still waiting for a call back," Tara said. "It's your big day. Don't worry about baseball or anything else except saying 'I do' to that gorgeous man of yours."

I smiled at her reference to Kade. I was marrying the hottest man in the world, and baseball could wait.

Besides, despite not playing ball, I was extremely happy with my life at the moment. Kade and I were designing our home on the lake, thanks to Mr. and Mrs. Maxwell's extraordinary wedding gift. Kade and his dad had worked out a deal on a mortgage payment. We would start out at a low monthly rate while Kade and I got on our feet. In the meantime, my soon-to-be husband and I were living at my dad's house. He wasn't charging us a dime to stay there, which gave us a chance to get our jobs and finances in order.

Becca crossed her arms over her chest, staring daggers at me.

"I got to run, Tara. I'll see you at the wedding."

After we said our goodbyes, Becca hooked her arm in mine. "Anything outside the wedding can wait. Give me your phone." She held out her free hand.

Reluctantly, I gave it to her. I didn't want to argue. She'd been the one person who was responsible for getting me to my big day without me pulling out my hair. We'd had several mishaps along the way too. The latest one had been the cake. The gal we hired had backed out at the last minute, like a week ago. So Becca, Mrs. Maxwell, and I had searched for a new one. But as it turned out, Kody had raised his hand to make the cake. He'd always been the one to bake cookies and other mouthwatering desserts.

We'd arched our eyebrows pretty high when he'd offered. Becca had protested at first, so Kody had baked a red velvet cake that was to die for. Kade and I didn't have any preferences on the type of cake. We just needed to have one to feed about a hundred guests.

Speaking of guests, family and mostly friends on all sides had accepted the invitation. Out of a hundred and thirty on the list, thirty had declined, including Tyler, who I'd invited.

"Do you know why Tyler isn't coming? Have you talked to him?" I asked as we made our way up to the Maxwell house. I'd always considered him a good friend. But before I sent the invitation, I'd asked Becca if she would be upset, and her response had been not at all.

She climbed up to the back deck ahead of me. "No and no." She sounded disappointed he wasn't coming.

When I reached the top step, I asked, "You still love him, don't you?"

Settling against the deck rail, she got this faraway look in her eyes. "I broke up with him."

I stood across from her, next to one of the high-back resin chairs. "That's not what I asked you."

A crease dented her forehead. "I caught him kissing another girl."

I reared back. "While he was dating you?" That was so unlike the Tyler I knew. Then again, the last time I'd seen Tyler was New Year's Eve two years ago, or maybe three. I couldn't remember. He and Becca had shown up at Rumors when Zeal played that night.

She sighed. "Yeah. I surprised him one weekend just before his graduation from Florida State." She fixated on the wooden planks we were standing on. "I showed up at a party, and lo and behold, he had his lips locked around some football cheerleader who'd been after him since he arrived on campus. I know it's shocking to hear that Tyler cheated on me, but he's different, Lace." She broke her stare. "In fact, he's not that sweet guy you knew in high school. I think his football stardom went to his head. Girls swarm all over him."

I imagine they did. Tyler was handsome, with blond hair and blue eyes and broad shoulders. Girls in high school had drooled over him.

I inclined my head. "You're leaving something out."

"We shouldn't be talking about Tyler. There's much to do before you walk down the red carpet. Besides, this is your day."

I rolled my eyes. "Maybe so, but that doesn't mean I don't have time to listen to my best friend. You'll feel better to get it off your chest. I know you've been holding in your feelings since you came home from college."

"I do love him." She got quiet for a beat. "But I'm an idiot for crushing on him since we were in grade school. It hurts, Lace, to have strong feelings for someone, but they don't have the same for you."

My heart broke for her. I could say there were other men out there or that she was beautiful and men should have been dropping to their knees for her, but she was still hurting. I could definitely see the pain in her eyes.

So I hugged her. "I'm sorry for all you've been through, and I wasn't there for you."

She gave me a squeeze. "Enough about Tyler and me. He and I will never be anyway, and I'm coming to terms with that. Right now"—she pointed to the slider—"let's go wake up some girls."

I puffed out my chest. "I'll only go in if I can call Kade." I had to hear his voice, and I was dying to find out about his time with Hunt and the guys.

She shook her pretty head but gave me my phone just the same. "Five minutes." Then she sashayed into the house.

I couldn't open my screen and tap his name in my favorites fast enough. When the line connected and his sexy morning voice came over the line, I hung my head.

"Hey, beautiful," he said. "I hear you're marrying some dude who is head over heels in love with you."

I beamed as bright as the sun. "He's okay," I teased.

"Baby, you better give me more than that, or else I'll be the one throwing you in the lake."

"Promise. We can skinny-dip tonight."

"How did you know that was on my list?" he asked so seriously.

"Great minds." I didn't know a thing. Our first night married would be spent in the boathouse before we headed off to Belize for our honeymoon, a wedding gift from my dad. Kade's parents had taken a vacation to Belize recently, and since Mrs. M. had spoken nonstop about the trip and shown us tons of pictures, I was hooked. "So how did your time go with Hunt?"

He chuckled. "Are you asking if we went all stripper-and-lap-dancing style?"

I growled a tad.

"Chill," he said through a laugh. "We did do something, but I'm not going to tell you."

Breathe, girl. He's just messing with you. But I didn't have the willpower to listen to the voice in my head. "Kade Maxwell, I swear if I find pictures of some girl on you or hear stories from your brothers or Hunt, I will kick you in the balls. And don't think I won't. Remember that day in high school in the janitor's closet when you tried to maul me."

He let out a belly laugh. "Baby, that was one of the best days of my life." His tone was dead serious. "Relax. Nothing of the sort happened. So are you ready to marry me?"

I went silent on purpose. If he was jerking my chain, then two could play that game.

"Lace." My name off his lips was sexy, but his tone screamed with a warning.

I sighed so heavily that I almost choked. Kade wouldn't allow any girl to touch him. But he would have to explain his night in detail later. "More than ready to tie the knot with the guy who sets me on fire," I said in a soft and serious tone. "I'm more than ready to make babies. More than ready to make love until the sun comes up or goes down. And more than ready to spend the rest of my life with you."

The line went silent as tears pricked my eyes. The emotions were starting, and I hoped I wouldn't be a blubbering mess through my vows.

"Kade."

"I'm here, baby. You just opened up my heart so fucking much. I can't wait to marry you."

My heart beat crazy wild, and the next four hours were going to tick by in slow motion.

CHAPTER 17
KADE

Kody, Kross, Kelton, and I held hands as we stood around Karen's memorial in a silent prayer. Forty-five minutes and counting until I married the woman of my dreams. A faint hum of music echoed from across the lake, where guests were arriving and ushers were seating them. The sun was almost high in the sky as it edged the top of the tree line that spanned the glassy lake.

My heart rammed so hard against my chest for so many reasons. I felt as though this day was my defining moment. My family and I had struggled since my sister's death. My mom had been in a mental health facility. Kody had lost his high school sweetheart to a motorcycle accident. Then he ended up almost dying himself from a brutal beating by my high school enemy, Greg Sullivan. I'd done a stint in jail when Kross and Kody took revenge on Sullivan. Then Lacey had been kidnapped and almost stabbed to death by some thug her estranged, fucked-up grandfather had hired, all to find the missing coordinates to buried money.

Despite all the bad in our lives, the last few years had slowly turned around with Mom coming home to live for good. Kelton had found the love of his life. Kross had not only found the girl he'd had feelings for since high school but had also learned he had a beautiful daughter, Raven. She certainly had been an eye-opener for all of us, and I couldn't imagine our family without her. Then Kody. Man, I hadn't thought my brother would get over the past. He'd mourned for his girl, Mandy, for so long until he'd met Jessie Ryan over a year ago.

I squeezed Kody's and Kross's hands. "Life would be complete if Karen were here."

"I miss her so fucking much," Kelton said, who stood on the other side of Kross.

"She would be how old now?" Kross asked.

Kody let go of me and wiped a tear away. "Twenty."

Our sister would have been beautiful and vibrant, and all of us would have probably grilled or killed the boy who stole her heart. "Let's recite her words," I said.

Karen had had a thing for hearts, and each one of us had her words memorized.

I began. "A beating heart is the mystery behind a person."

My brothers joined in.

"When people hurt, their hearts hurt," we said. "When they love, their hearts love, and when they cry, their hearts cry too. The heart knows everything."

We each took in an audible breath.

"Amen," we said in unison.

I checked my watch. Thirty-five minutes, and I would be a married man.

Kody fixed the cuff of his shirt beneath his tux. "Kade?"

I rubbed my hand over the initials KM etched on the rock. "Yeah, man."

"Thank you for being the big brother. Thank you for making sure I didn't go nuts all these years," Kody said.

Kross gripped my shoulder briefly. "You've always been there for us."

Kelton blinked rapidly as if trying to stave off tears. "I second all that. Our lives are changing. I can't say that I'm not a little freaked out by what the future holds because I am. I don't want us going our separate ways. I want us to stay together, to have our brothers-only nights, to hang out on the lake like we did as teenagers."

Well, fuck.

Kelton was about to make me emotional. "Listen. We're getting older. We're building our families. But don't think for a minute that we're not together." I touched my heart. "We're in here. We'll have houses on the lake." I waved my hand around at all the land my parents had purchased. "This is our home. It will always be, from here on out."

Kody tucked a hand in his pants pocket. "I'm not moving anywhere. Ashford is where I'll stay. Mom and Dad aren't going anywhere, either."

Kross grabbed his bow tie on his tux, his blue eyes cloudy. "I'm not boxing forever. I have two kids now and want a ton more. I want them to grow up here. I want them to have the best life I can give them. So I've decided to open up a training facility in Ashford in the next couple of years."

Kelton, Kody, and I reared back. That was news, great news.

"I'll help you in any way I can." I had my job at the Cave, but I had long-term plans to do more like restore old cars. In the meantime, if Lacey did sign with a baseball team, then I would follow her, but Ashford was home.

Kelton gave us one of his famous cocky smirks. "Maybe I can open up a law office in town. Lizzie is dying to get married and have kids."

Kelton was studying criminal law. So I wasn't sure that a small town like Ashford would have many clients since our crime rate was rather low. Nevertheless, my heart burst wide open.

The four of us turned and glanced out over the lake. In the distance, people sat waiting for the ceremony to begin, while others stood around chatting.

"We should get back." I didn't want the moment to end, but I also didn't want to miss my wedding.

Kody and Kelton started ahead of Kross and me.

"Kade, how's your head?" Kross asked. "Any headaches as of late?"

Kody and Kelton each tossed a look over his shoulder but kept walking, although at a slower pace.

"I haven't had any migraines since before the operation. In fact, I've gotten a clean bill of health from Dr. Thompson." After the surgery, I'd spent more time sleeping and trying to get over how tired I'd felt more than anything.

My brothers released a sigh of relief as we wound our way through the tree-laden path around the lake. When we emerged into the open space of where the guests were tittering and chatting and music was playing, my brothers scattered.

I did one sweep of the backyard, which had been transformed into a palace of flowers, tents, and tables, reminding me of an event designed for a king and queen. I grinned. Lacey was my queen, goddess, lover, best friend, soon-to-be wife, the mother of my future children, and the only woman who could make my heart flutter, race, and stop all at the same time.

I was hoping to get a glimpse of my bride. Instead, I spotted Hunt talking to my dad at the spot where Lacey and I would say I do.

I strutted up to Hunt and my dad. As I did, I passed relatives and friends, who waved and smiled. I wanted to stop and talk to my cousins, whom I hadn't seen in years, but I would have plenty of time to talk with them later. Right now, I had to try and quiet my pulse and make sure Hunt had the wedding bands.

Hunt flicked his chin at me. His usually wild mess of blond hair didn't move today, thanks in part to lots of gel. It was rather unusual to see him all decked out in a tux rather than his casual dress of jeans and a company-logo golf shirt that he wore on his job at the security firm.

I stepped up on the small wooden platform. "Hey, Dad. Are you ready?" My dad was marrying us.

We were Catholic, but Lacey wasn't, and I wasn't that much of a devout Catholic. So we had decided to keep things simple. Kross had asked Kelton, Kody, and me to marry him and Ruby. So I didn't want to break the chain, so to speak. I'd thought about my brothers marrying us, but Lacey wanted them as groomsmen. My mom wanted that too. She'd also hoped we would at least get married in the church, but Lacey and I had agreed that wasn't our choice. So I'd asked my dad to marry us. That request had made my mom so much happier. Besides, my dad had been and still was my hero. I couldn't see anyone else joining Lacey and me in marriage.

He swept his copper gaze over me with a grin the size of the moon. "I've been ready for this day, son, since you were born."

I inclined my head at my dad, who looked rather debonair in his black tux, with his styled graying hair and clean-shaven face.

"I'm proud of you, Kade," Dad said. "You've turned into the man I always thought you would be—strong, determined, protective, and you have so much love in your heart. You remind me so much of myself."

I stood taller. "Um... I am your son," I teased.

The three of us chuckled.

Dad met me eye to eye. "In all seriousness, your mom and I can't be happier for you and Lacey."

I swallowed down the sentimental lump I had at the base of my throat.

Dad glanced at his watch. "Ten minutes before we begin. I need to get my notes. I'll be right back." He hurried off, darting past the ushers, who were escorting the last of the guests to their seats.

I'd asked Dillon Hart and two of his buddies to help out with seating guests. I'd even asked Mack Donovan. He'd been one of our enemies in high school, and now he was a family friend. Kody and he had worked out their differences, and Kross, Kelton, and I had flushed out the pent-up ire we'd had for him too. He had turned out to be a super dude, who had nothing but love in his heart, especially for my mom.

Hunt pulled on his shirtsleeves. "Did you tell Lacey what you did in Boston?"

"Hell no. She'll find out soon enough. By the way, do you have the rings?" It was probably a little late to be asking.

"Of course," Hunt said.

I tossed a look over my shoulder toward the garage, where Lacey would emerge when the ceremony began. I wanted to see her so badly.

Hunt nudged me. "You'll see her soon enough. Now think of something else. Your hands are shaking."

I almost laughed. I couldn't think of anything else but Lacey. Slipping my hands into my pants pockets, I eyed the lake. Flowers floated by, and my mind wandered.

The high school parking lot was dark with barely any lights spraying around the lot. I searched high and low for Kelton, who'd taken off after a brotherly spat we'd had. I was worried he would do something stupid like find Greg Sullivan and beat the shit out of him. Revenge was high on his list after Sullivan and his buddies had beat Kody into a coma. Regardless, my search for Kelton died when I spotted her, alone at her car with no one around. Normally, I would've kept to myself, but moments before that, I'd seen how she pitched, graceful yet tough. I was in awe. So I couldn't help but introduce myself. I banged on the trunk of her car, more to alert her than scare her.

She emerged from the driver's side with a gun in her hand, pointing it at me with fire in her green eyes. I knew she wouldn't shoot me. Still, I backed away, telling her to put the gun away. We exchanged words back and forth until the stadium light went out, throwing the lot into darkness. Then I made my move. Within thirty seconds, I was standing so close to her, I could smell her citrus scent, which sent my groin into overdrive. Not to mention, she was feisty, with an attitude that screamed "don't fuck with me." That alone was so darn sexy that I knew she was the girl for me.

Hunt's voice was in my ear, severing my trip down memory lane. "Dude, you're going to miss your bride."

I blinked as my dad walked up with his notes in his hands. My brothers scurried up to stand next to Hunt.

Kody raised his hand at his girl, Jessie. She stood on the temporary stage behind the guests and the tables and chairs that were scattered around under the large tents. She hit a key on the laptop.

Violin music, soft and elegant, filtered out of the large speakers set up on each end of the stage. The trees rustled as if it were their cue to chime in.

My heart danced endlessly as Raven walked down first. She smiled from ear to ear as she held a white wicker basket in one hand and dropped white rose petals with her other.

In a low voice, Kross said, "Damn, I have a beautiful daughter."

He sure did. She looked so much like my mom, it was uncanny. Nevertheless, she bounced down the red carpet. When she reached the platform, she handed the basket to my mom. Then she curtsied, smiling at me before she took her seat in between my mom and her mom, Ruby, who was holding her daughter Reaghan.

"You did well," my mom said to Raven.

Ruby leaned in close to her daughter. "You were great."

Raven cooed as she sat up straighter.

I tore my gaze away from Raven to find Jennifer walking down first. She was the same woman who had tried to help me that day outside of Lacey's dorm when she thought I needed help. She held a bouquet of white roses in front of her red strapless gown as she slowly walked down to stand on the platform to my dad's right.

Next up was Heather, who wore the same style gown as Jennifer. Where Jennifer had short brown hair, Heather had blond hair that was piled up on her head. She was also carrying the same type of bouquet as Jennifer.

Once she was settled next to Jennifer, Peggy stepped up. Again, she had the same style of dress and flowers. Peggy winked at me, her hazel eyes filled with excitement as she joined her friends.

Right on Peggy's heels was Becca, dressed in a black halter gown that looked to be the same fabric as the other bridesmaids' attire. She was also carrying white roses.

With my heart beating like the heavy bass of a rock song, I fixated on the spot to the left of the garage.

I spotted Lacey's old man first, holding out his elbow. Then I took in a huge breath as Lacey came into view.

Holy fuck.

I swayed on my feet.

This was it. I was about to say I do.

I fidgeted.

"You're not breathing, man," Hunt whispered.

I couldn't. The most stunning woman stood several yards from me, and all I wanted to do was run to her.

The guests rose from their seats.

My hands shook.

Lacey glanced up at her dad as she hooked her arm in his. He clutched Lacey's hand as if she would turn and run at any moment.

I closed my eyes briefly, praying she wouldn't run. *She won't. Get a grip, dude.*

They walked, or more like shuffled, toward us.

My heart was all over the map.

The closer she came to me, the more my body shook, rattled, and rolled.

My dad slid over to me. "Son," he whispered, "you're turning pale. Think of your honeymoon."

I swished some saliva around in my mouth, and I did what my old man had suggested. I tuned out the music and the crowd and focused on all the things I had planned for my bride and me that night and when we were in Belize. Sex, sleep, and eat. Repeat.

Lacey and her dad settled just on the edge of the red carpet where it met the wooden deck. Then he lifted her veil, kissed her on the cheek, and grabbed her hand. "You are the most beautiful bride I've ever seen. Your mom and sister would be so in awe of how you turned out. It's time to start that new chapter in your life."

She placed her small hand in his large one as he ushered her up to me.

I couldn't take my eyes off her. Her sleeveless dress was cut low, almost down to her waist, where it was cinched with a large diamond buckle. Her hair was twisted up in a fancy style with thin strands of hair neatly curled and framing her face. Her makeup was light yet perfectly done. The light-green eye shadow made her eyes stand out more.

She batted long lashes, giving me a shy yet seductive look. A chill shimmied up my arm as warmth danced down my stomach. If I didn't know Lacey, I would say she wasn't as nervous as me. But I knew her tells, and she held her bottom lip hostage.

Mr. Robinson gave me his daughter's hand. "I know, Kade, that you'll take good care of her." Then he excused himself and went to sit across the aisle from my mom in one of three empty seats.

Mr. Robinson didn't have to worry about his daughter. I would never let anything happen to her, even if it meant my life for hers.

Lacey squeezed my hand.

Dad cleared his throat.

"Focus on me," Lacey said in a wobbly voice.

I had no problem keeping my gaze on her. I had to if I didn't want to pass out. So with that, I took in a breath and gave my beautiful bride my undivided attention.

CHAPTER 18
LACEY

I stared at Kade. My heart warmed, and my soul blossomed. Even though he was breathing heavy as though he were trying to catch his breath, he gave me one of his sexiest grins, showing the dimples I so loved.

We joined hands, and instantly it felt as though a bright light flashed, all voices ceased, and we were transported to a faraway place.

"I'm as nervous as you," I whispered.

Becca grabbed my bouquet.

A breeze swept over us.

My pulse began to slow, more so when Kade took my other hand and kissed the back of it. "You're absolutely stunning." His gaze dropped to the low neckline then back up.

His dad cleared his throat.

It was now or never, and I wanted to marry Kade so badly that I swung my gaze to Mr. Maxwell. When our eyes met, it was as though I was looking at the older version of Kade—handsome, strong, and powerful. All those attributes described the elder Maxwell as well as his son.

I could see our children resembling the patriarch side of the Maxwell family—tall, honey-brown hair, and copper eyes that were kind, sweet, and caring.

Mr. Maxwell blinked with a smile then turned to his son.

Carnations floated on the smooth surface of the water, and most of the flowers had fanned out since the florist had tossed them in that morning.

"Today is a special day." Mr. Maxwell addressed the guests, or maybe he was looking at his wife. "A spectacular day." He tapped his chest then fixated on Kade and me. "My heart is so full right now. Marriage is not only the union of the love for each other, but a journey that you both will take together. The bond you share is not only in sickness and in health. It's in the good moments and bad. It's in family. Support each other. Love each other. Take care of each other. Make decisions together, and build a life that you both want for you and your children." He paused for a brief second. "Now, Lacey, do you have your vows?"

I nodded at Mr. Maxwell, trying to shake the cobwebs from my brain in the hope that I wouldn't screw up.

I rubbed my lips together as I pivoted on my heel. I checked on my dad and the two empty seats next to him. I knew it sounded crazy, but since Julie and Mom weren't physically there, I wanted the idea of them to be. I'd felt their spirit at the cemetery and wanted to have the same feeling at my wedding. Kade and the rest of the family hadn't even flinched when I said I wanted to keep two seats empty next to my dad. My dad didn't even question my sanity. All he'd said was "That's a great idea, sweet pea."

So I pushed out the air in my lungs, nodded at my dad, closed my eyes briefly, and said silently, "I love you, Julie. I love you, Mom."

Then I turned to Kade. I swallowed thickly as Hunt gave me Kade's wedding band. I had vows. I'd written out words, but suddenly I couldn't even think.

I frantically searched my brain for words, but I came up empty. If people were talking or whispering, I couldn't hear them.

Say what you're feeling. Tell the man you love that it's always been him. Oddly, the old man I'd spoken to at the cemetery in LA materialized in my head, as did a warm feeling of comfort as though my mom and Julie were there. I could feel my eyebrows coming together as I remembered the old man's words. "Make sure you put your loved ones before anything else."

The tips of Kade's fingers touched the underside of my chin. "Baby, you're not panicking?" A tinge of fear swam in his eyes.

I knew I should speak. I knew I should do something before Kade thought I was getting cold feet or heading for one of my famous blackouts.

Kade leaned in slightly. "I love the crap out of you."

I giggled, and all sense of confusion began to clear.

He straightened.

I fumbled with the ring. I still couldn't remember my vows. But I did know that all I had to convey was how much I loved Kade Maxwell. As the nervous nellies feasted inside me, I said the first thing that came to me. "Kade." I snuck a peek at my dad and the empty chairs beside him. Then I set my sights on the man who made my heart race. "Kade," I said again. "My mom always told my dad that he was the best thing that ever happened to her. When I asked her why, she said, 'Because your father is delicate with my heart, soft with his hands, and wraps me in hugs every night.' You are the man I've always dreamed about marrying. You are delicate with my heart. You're strong. You're protective, and you have so much love to give. I can't wait for you to wrap me in your hugs every night." I slipped the ring on his finger. "You're the best thing that has ever happened to me. I am yours forever."

His chest rose and fell at huge proportions.

Hunt then gave Kade my diamond-studded wedding band to match my diamond setting.

He slid the band over my ring finger.

My pulse began to slow.

Kade then took both my hands in his. "Before I met you, I never thought I would meet a woman who would capture my heart like you did." His tone was calm, confident, and full of love as we locked eyes. "I never thought I would ever settle down. When I laid eyes on you for the first time was the day my life took a turn I didn't see coming. Since then, I couldn't imagine my life without you. You make me a better man, a lover, and friend. I will be true to you. I will be the husband my father raised me to be. I will be the husband who will protect you, love you, and die for you." He touched his heart. "This is yours until my last breath."

Tears were streaming down my face. Soft cries could be heard in the background.

I tried to catch my breath.

"You are officially husband and wife," Mr. Maxwell said.

Kade's lips were on mine before Mr. Maxwell said anything else.

Cheers and whistles peppered the air.

Kade's strong arm went around my waist, drawing me to his hard body as he shoved his tongue in my mouth.

I was waiting for someone, like Kelton, to shout get a room. Instead, Kade's father spoke. "All right, Mr. and Mrs. Maxwell."

Hearing him call us Mr. and Mrs. made me giggle.

As hard as it was for me to let go, I took a step back, and we separated.

Kade plastered on a smirk that sent lots of heat south. "Man, that sounds awesome. Are you okay now, Mrs. Kade Maxwell?"

Mrs. Kade Maxwell sounded even better coming from him. I giggled more. It seemed so surreal that Kade and I had come so far.

His dad slapped a hand on his son's back. "Congratulations."

Kade threw his arms around his father. "Thank you so much."

Becca came up and hugged me. "I can't stop crying. Congrats, bestie."

Then like a swarm of bees, people were congratulating us. Kade got lost in the crowd. I was sucked up by my dad, who was holding me so tight I couldn't breathe. I was a bit sad, though, that my brother, Rob, had missed my wedding. He was somewhere around the world, trying to find himself. He'd said he would make it up to me when he returned next year.

After all the congrats and kisses from family and friends, our photographer corralled the wedding party for pictures, while the guests sipped champagne and listened to music.

About an hour later, my mouth hurt from smiling so much. I wanted to find a quiet place and take a nap before the reception, but I only got married once, and I wanted to celebrate no matter how tired I was.

Our family and friends were laughing and talking when Kade and I arrived hand in hand.

Jessie, who was dressed in a soft peach sundress, stood on stage with a microphone in hand. "Ladies and gentlemen, I would like to introduce you to Mr. and Mrs. Kade Maxwell." She flicked her multi-colored hair off her bare shoulder as she nodded at us.

Cheers, applause, and whistles greeted us as we walked over to the dance floor.

Then Kody picked up his guitar. Jake Trent twirled a drumstick in his hand as he got behind the drum set. Jennifer squealed from the sidelines, as did Heather. They were crushing on the green-eyed hunk, who I'd known for quite some time. He'd managed his brother JJ's band, Zeal—the same band my dad had signed to his old record label.

The song Kade and I picked started.

Kade wrapped an arm around my waist, took my hand, and brought it to his chest. When we'd been planning the wedding, I asked him if he could dance. He'd rolled his eyes at me then turned on the radio. The song that had been playing was "The Rest of Our Life," by Tim McGraw and Faith Hill. The words were perfect for us.

Jessie sang, "Sitting with you in a dark room. Warmed by the fireplace. You know there's just something about you. You brightened my day."

Kade's feet moved, then I was dancing with him. Our gazes were glued to each other.

Jessie's voice was melodic as she sang the words, and when she got to the lyrics "I've been making plans for children. Since I've been looking in your eyes. I even have names picked out for them," sad tears slipped down my face as Julie and Mom came to mind.

Kade brought me closer to him, cradling our hands in between us. "What do you think of Julie for a girl's name?" he whispered in my ear.

I cried harder. I'd never told him I wanted to name a girl Julie if we had a daughter.

He hugged me tighter to him. "Shh. I know you miss your mom and sister. I miss Karen. How about we make your mom and sister a memorial in our backyard like we did for Karen?"

I craned my neck up, tears flowing. "I would love that."

He swiped his fingers over my cheeks.

As the song was ending, the wedding party joined us on the dance floor.

Becca waltzed over with Hunt. Her black halter-style bodice that clasped around her neck with sheer fabric covering the area from her breasts to her neckline complemented her bluish-black hair and long neck. Hunt had a grin on his face as though he was pleased to have a beautiful lady on his arm.

Peggy and Kross joined us next. Peggy, along with Heather and Jennifer, wore a slightly different style gown than Becca. All the gowns had crisscross bodices made out of chiffon, but instead of the halter neckline, the bridesmaid dresses were strapless and red.

Jennifer and Kelton danced on the other side of Kade and me. I was about to search for Heather and motion for her to join us even though she didn't have a partner since Kody was on stage, but she glided up like an angel with a huge smile on her face and Dillon Hart at her side.

144

I could see why she was smitten. I hadn't seen Dillon in a long time, and even though he was still sporting his almost-shoulder-length brown hair, he had grown in a nice close-shaven beard that made him look like more of a badass. And if I remembered correctly, Dillon loved blondes, and Heather was blond and beautiful.

All my bridesmaids were gorgeous and the sweetest women I knew.

"Thank you." I pinned a look on the girls, and even the guys, in the wedding party.

Kade chimed in. "We're grateful that you are in our lives."

Jessie sang her popular song, "Dare to Live," that had gotten a lot of traction on the radio.

More guests joined us on the dance floor.

Then someone tapped me on the shoulder. "Can I have this dance?"

I froze.

Kade stepped back with a huge grin, waving his hand for Rob to take his place.

When my brother came into view, I jumped into his arms. Well, I tried to. It was hard to do much in a wedding dress.

Rob wrapped his arms around me. "I wouldn't have missed this day for the world."

"I thought you were somewhere across the ocean." I could never keep track of where he was.

Out of the corner of my eye, I spied Kade snagging his mom and pulling her onto the dance floor. Mrs. Maxwell was as pretty and elegant as ever, dressed in a royal-blue tea-length dress that hugged her curves and sat slightly off her shoulders.

Rob let go of me and combed his fingers through his wavy brown hair. "Dad and I wanted to surprise you."

I beamed like a kid in a candy store. "Best surprise ever."

Or at least I thought it was until I spotted Tara with her friend. I did a double take when I saw John Gleason, the scout for the Red Sox. I didn't know they were dating.

John regarded me with his kind brown eyes.

Rob followed my line of sight. "John Gleason?"

I swallowed, nodding. Rob knew John from his days in the major leagues.

"Sis, did you sign with the Red Sox?"

I jerked my head at my brother. "Not at all. The lady with him, Tara Bannister, is my agent."

Tara and John stopped dancing next to Rob and me.

Tara extended her hand to Rob. "Tara Bannister."

"Rob Robinson," my brother said.

Tara flipped her brunette hair over her shoulder. "I know who you are. It's sad you decided to stop playing baseball."

"Well, I'm here to celebrate my sister's wedding, not talk about baseball." My brother would always deflect the attention away from him and onto others. He'd never liked the spotlight, either.

Then John and Rob exchanged a handshake.

The song stopped.

"We're going to take a break," Jessie said.

People scattered off the dance floor with the exception of John, Tara, Rob, and me.

Kade strutted over. "What's going on?"

Kade had met Tara when she'd come into town several months back to talk to me just before I'd signed with her.

Kade draped an arm around me.

Glasses clinked, and voices peppered the air as everyone settled in, ready to eat.

"Before you're scooped up with all the wedding activities," Tara said, "I wanted to share some good news with you."

My pulse sped up. News from Tara meant that a major league team could be interested in me. I eyed John, who was smirking.

Tara tipped her chin at John.

The man rubbed his hand down his dark-red tie. "After many meetings and conversations, the Red Sox would like to offer you a relief pitching position with the Portland Sea Dogs. You would start after the All-Star break."

I clutched my chest. "Are you serious?" The Sea Dogs were a Double-A team within the Sox organization, and they were based in Maine, which meant I would be close to home.

Kade squeezed me to him. "She'll sign."

I whipped my head up at him, not that I was mad he'd spoken for me, but I was a little shocked that he wanted me to go. We had our honeymoon to think about, although I had over a month before I would start playing.

He leaned down to my ear. "Say yes."

"Yes," I shouted. I couldn't contain my excitement. Even though it wasn't the big leagues, I was beyond excited to get to play baseball. Besides, it was a place to start my climb up. If I did well, then the management team would see that, and maybe one day, I would be pitching with the big boys.

For now, I couldn't have asked for a more perfect man, day, and life. My brother was there. My dad was happy with his new recording studio. Kade was healthy, and so was I. Above all else, I was Mrs. Kade Maxwell, and Kade and me and our love for one another trumped anything and anyone, including baseball.

CHAPTER 19
KADE

The lake area that had been buzzing with laughter, excitement, dancing, and music was now quiet except for the crickets.

The late-night air held a thin layer of humidity, or maybe my body was overheated, anticipating that moment when I carried Lacey over the threshold.

We climbed the steps up to the boathouse, hand in hand. I could almost feel her pulse beating against my sweaty palm. Lacey reached out for the doorknob.

"Wait," I said.

I wanted nothing more than to get inside and get naked. Man, I'd been dying to do just that when I saw her in her wedding dress, which she was still wearing.

Her long lashes swept down over her cheeks. The illuminated deck and the moon shining provided more than ample light to see how her face was a shade of rose from the blush she was wearing.

I caged her in between the door and my body, studying her,

absorbing her citrus scent that had driven me mad all day. Her breathing slowly ramped up.

I debated whether to suggest skinny-dipping, but the lake water was rather cold. Earlier, as guests were leaving, I'd checked the temperature real quick. Sadly, the boathouse didn't have a shower or a tub where we could lather each other up or relax in a warm bath.

Her tongue snaked out. "I'm not afraid to go in."

My body was humming as I watched her lick her bottom lip. "My brothers decorated the place. Are you sure about that?" I had no idea what they'd done to the inside. Frankly, as long as a bed existed, I was fine with whatever would jump out at us.

Her answer wasn't with words. Instead, she found Mr. Steel. "Mmm. Does anything else matter?"

My eyes rolled back in my head as she rubbed her hand along my dick. I fumbled with the doorknob.

Laughing, she let go of Mr. Steel, and I fucking whimpered.

She was about to dash inside, but I caught her arm. "Wait one second, Mrs. Maxwell." I lifted her in my arms. "I need to carry my bride over the threshold."

She locked her hands around my neck as I stepped into a room lit with candles.

"Mm," she muttered, wiggling down out of my arms.

The room was jam-packed not only with candles but with flowers. The fragrant aroma permeated the air.

"I caught Kelton slipping into the boathouse about an hour ago. He must've lit the candles," I mumbled.

Lacey walked around, smelling the lilies and roses.

I closed and locked the door before padding over to the bed, where a note sat mysteriously underneath one long-stem rose. I snagged the white piece of paper then read aloud, "Hey, bro and Mrs. M. I bet you two thought we would prank the joint. Well, we wouldn't call it a prank, but if you're reading this note, then you're near the bed. So look up."

Lacey slowly lifted her gaze. I hesitated, praying it wasn't some sort of joke, although I had no idea what prank they could pull from the ceiling.

Lacey broke out in a fit of laughter.

So I looked up and saw myself in the mirror that was tacked to the ceiling.

I glanced down at the note. "Pretty kinky, huh?" I read aloud.

Lacey inched over and flopped on the bed. "I like it. I'll be able to watch you better."

At that thought, my tuxedo pants became impossibly tight.

Her watching me. Me watching her.

Fuck.

I couldn't get my clothes off fast enough. But I slowed to a halt when I started to unbutton my shirt, remembering what I'd done while Hunt, my brothers, and I were in Boston. "I have a surprise for you."

Sitting up, she yawned.

Then I yawned.

She laughed. I did too.

The anticipation of this moment had been on my mind all fucking day. Now we were both ready to fall asleep. Well, that was not happening.

She adjusted herself so she was on her knees at the edge of the bed. "I'll undress you. What's the surprise?"

I went quiet.

She lifted her gaze to me. "Cat got your tongue?"

Nope. I unpinned her hair and let the strands fall around her. My balls tightened at the sight of how fucking gorgeous she was.

She abandoned my shirt for my belt.

I finished her task and removed my shirt then T-shirt. She had just gotten my belt off and was working on my zipper, when her eyes flickered up my chest.

Her jaw came unhinged as she examined the bandage over my heart with her fingers. "Kade Maxwell, who hurt you?"

I chuckled. "Take off the bandage."

She did, albeit slowly. When the bandage was gone, she squealed. "Are you for real? Is that what you did in Boston?"

I twirled a clump of her hair with my fingers. "I told you in our vows. My heart is yours forever."

She gently traced the outline of my new heart tattoo that sat above the other four. Only this heart had her name inked inside of it.

"I love it." She grasped the waist of my pants and tried to pull me to her.

I hesitated. "First, the dress needs to come off."

I would like to say that our clothes were off in a flash. But with the intricate way the back of her dress was clasped together, it took us five minutes before we were both naked, and she was straddling me in the candlelit room.

I glanced up in the mirror, and my body fired into action. I clutched her hips as she sank down on my dick.

I sucked in a sharp breath. "Not wasting any time."

Her tongue darted out then back in as she rocked her toned body up then down. Just watching her in the mirror was enough for me to orgasm. But I couldn't. I wanted to take my time. I wanted to enjoy every fucking moment, minute, hour, day, year, and forever with her having her way with me.

She moaned as her breasts bounced.

I rubbed a path up the sides of her curves until I was pinching her nipples.

She mewled louder. "Kade, I'm not going to last."

I flipped us, pulling her off me. "You're not letting go yet."

She pouted. "Why? We can go round two, three, four, and so on all night long."

She had a point, and holding out would be painful. Regardless, I had to taste her. I would never forget how explosive our first time had been. Over the years, our lovemaking had actually gotten more powerful than when we were in high school. I would never get tired of her body. Never.

I settled in between her legs, and as if on cue, she opened for me. I kissed the inside of one thigh then the other, trailing my lips up. Her breathing grew shallow, and when I captured her bundle of nerves, she shot off the bed.

I reached up and flattened my hand on her stomach, urging her to lie back.

"Kade, you have to stop. I want you inside me first," she protested.

As an answer, I sucked her clit into my mouth and swirled my tongue around. In a second, she was writhing and moaning and saying my name over and over again. When I pushed a finger inside her, she tensed before she gripped the sheets. I let her ride out her orgasm as I crawled up her body and positioned my dick at her entrance.

My own breathing increased as adrenaline shot through me. At that moment with the soft light, us, and her as my wife, the world spun even more when I said, "Mrs. Kade Maxwell."

She squirmed as her hands clutched Mr. Steel. Then she guided me as we locked eyes. I thrust in slow and steady.

She glanced up at the ceiling. I did too, but I couldn't exactly see that well.

Her lips formed into a seductive grin as I pushed all the way into her. She swung her arms out to the sides of the bed and kept her eyes on the mirror as I moved in and out. The thought of her watching me only made me move faster, harder.

She rocked with me as she played with her nipples.

"Legs around me," I commanded.

Sweat dripped from me onto her.

When her ankles were locked around me, she squeezed, her inner walls gripping me so hard, I growled. I didn't want this moment to end. But my body had a mind of its own. One more thrust, and I was a goner. Stars coated my vision as I rocked one last time before that free-falling sensation overtook my body.

I peered down at her. "Unconscious beauty." I'd said those two words to her many times in high school. She had a way of walking into a room, poised and confident, turning heads and totally unaware of the effects she had on the opposite sex.

She shivered as she continued to grip my dick. "I love you, husband."

I captured her earlobe in my mouth. "You are my unconscious beauty. My life has never been as complete as it is now. Now if you keep squeezing, round two won't be long."

She squealed. "Good. I don't want to stop until the sun comes up."

Unfortunately, I needed to regroup. My little minx was full of vigor for someone who'd appeared to be sleepy only twenty minutes ago.

I rolled off her, and she whimpered.

I ran my hand through my sweaty hair.

She lifted up on her elbow then lightly touched my new tattoo. "Does your chest hurt from the tattoo?"

Until that moment, I hadn't registered any pain, but a dull ache began to surface, which didn't matter.

All that did matter was her and me and the life we were about to build together.

DEAR READER

When I started to write the first book in this series, Dare to Kiss, I had no idea how well the book would do. Six books later and readers from all over the world are in love with the Maxwells. I can't tell you how happy that makes me. Thank you for taking a chance on me and for loving the Maxwell men.

I've been asked many times if there will be more Maxwell books, and while I do have a couple of storylines in mind, I can't say for sure when any more books in this series will be released.

What I can say is that you will see books on some of the secondary characters that you've met throughout the series. And first up will be Hart of Darkness. This story is based on Dillon Hart as he embarks on a crusade to find his baby sister.

Books in the Maxwell Series
Dare to Kiss - Kade Maxwell's story
Dare to Dream - Kade Maxwell's story continued
Dare to Love - Kelton Maxwell's story
Dare to Dance - Kross Maxwell's story
Dare to Live - Kody Maxwell's story
Dare to Breathe - Kade Maxwell's story

Dare to Kiss and Dare to Dream should be read in order.

However, Dare to Love, Dare to Dance, and Dare to Live can all be read as a stand alone.

Dare to Breathe should be read after reading Dare to Kiss and Dare to Dream.

Also, if you have moment to spare, I would super appreciate a short review. Your help in sharing your excitement and spreading the word about the Maxwell brothers would be greatly appreciated.

CONNECT WITH ME

facebook.com/sbalexander.authorpage

twitter.com/sbalex_author

instagram.com/sbalexanderauthor

amazon.com/author/sbalexander

bookbub.com/authors/s-b-alexander

TITLES BY S.B. ALEXANDER

To read samples and find out where to purchase all books visit:
http://sbalexander.com/books

The Maxwell Series:

Dare to Kiss - Book 1

Dare to Dream – Book 2

Dare to Love – Book 3

Dare to Dance - Book 4

Dare to Live - Book 5

Dare to Breathe - Book 6

The Maxwell Series Boxed Set – Books 1-3

Dare to Kiss Coloring Book Companion

The Vampire SEAL Series:

On the Edge of Humanity – Book 1

On the Edge of Eternity – Book 2

On the Edge of Destiny – Book 3

On the Edge of Misery - Book 4
On the Edge of Infinity - Book 5
The Vampire SEAL Collection - Boxed Set

A Stand Alone Novel
Breaking Rules

ACKNOWLEDGMENTS

I want to thank my fans, readers, bloggers, Indie Sage PR Company, and my dedicated ARC team. I'm humbled by all the reviews, messages, and your help in spreading the word about my books. Hugs and kisses to each and every one of you for taking the time to take this journey with me and sharing your excitement.

To everyone in Maxwell Mania, I love the crap out of you. Thank you for loving the series, and the Maxwell boys. Most of all, thank you for spreading the word. Your excitement means more than you know.

The team at Red Adept Editing is without a doubt the best editing team in the industry.

An enormous thank you to the talented Hang Le for her creativity and book cover design. You're absolutely amazing.

To the gals in the wedding party, Jennifer, Peggy, and Heather: hugs and kisses.

A big shout out to the beta team— Kylie Sharp, Terri Schorr, and Heather Carver, much love and thanks for all your help.

Amy Korbel, Jennifer Lowe, and Heather Carver thank you for all your help and support in Maxwell Mania.

Kylie Sharp, where do I begin. You've talked me down off a few ledges, and I can't thank you enough for being there for me not only in the book world, but in our personal lives as well. You and your family are near and dear to my heart. Bill and I love you guys.

Finally, to the man who stole my heart. I love you more than you know.